AMISH TWIN TROUBLE

A ROMANTIC SUSPENSE NOVELLA

AMISH DETECTIVE BENUEL MILLER
BOOK ONE

RACHEL J. GOOD

PRAYERFUL PRODUCTIVITY

ISBN: 978-1-63888-010-3 (ebook), 978-1-63888-011-0 (print)

CHAPTER 1

$\mathcal{T}$he bells over the door of Benuel Miller's secondhand shop jingled, and a customer entered. From his tentative steps, the man—definitely a man, judging by his heavy footfalls—was both a stranger and an *Englischer*.

Without turning from the items he was pricing, Benuel said, "Welcome. Since you haven't been here before, used furniture's in the basement, clothing's on the second floor, kitchenware and household goods are in the next room."

He didn't need to point out the books, toys, and miscellaneous items in this room. The man could see those for himself. "Oh, and gardening equipment, plants, and outdoor furniture are under the canopy out back."

The man's steps faltered. He probably wondered how Benuel had pegged him as a newcomer without even looking at him.

"Um, thanks," the man said and headed up the stairs. He returned a short while later with a small pile of clothing.

Rubbing his fingers over the price tags, Benuel mentally calculated the total. *Interesting.* The *Englisher* had selected Amish pants, suspenders, and a short-sleeved shirt, along

1

with a straw hat. The clothing prices indicated two things—the man was used to higher quality clothing and he had money. He'd chosen the newest and best of their stock.

Benuel fingered the two bills the customer had just handed him. "Two twenties?" he guessed.

"Yes." The *Englischer* standing on the other side of the counter twitched and shuffled from one foot to the other.

Though Benuel couldn't see the man, waves of impatience radiated from his body, along with the smell of fear. This stranger had no trace of the Amish *Deutsch* accent most of his secondhand shop customers had. In fact, his accent was quite distinct, at least to Benuel's ears. Benuel slipped the twenties into the correct slot in the cash register, then slid coins into one hand and rifled swiftly through the fives and ones with the other to give his customer the correct change.

"How did you do that?" The man's astonishment—and a bit of wariness—crept into his words.

"Do what?" Benuel pretended he had no idea what the man meant, although he did.

"Making change like that. And so quickly when you can't see."

"My fingers work just fine, and so does my brain." For some reason, people often talked down to him because he was blind. Regular customers had learned not to underestimate him.

"You're not from around here," Benuel remarked as he counted the quarters, dimes, and pennies into the man's hand. "New Jersey, right?"

The floorboards creaked as the man took a step back. Most strangers were astonished when Benuel placed them correctly. This man would be even more amazed if he knew all the other clues Benuel had picked up about him. The man's height from the angle of his hand as he'd reached

2

down to extend the money and his approximate weight from the press of his footsteps.

Benuel had brushed his fingers lightly over the man's outstretched hand before he dropped the change into it. The stranger likely attributed the fumbling to blindness, but Benuel could have placed the change precisely into the man's palm. He had his reasons for the faked clumsiness. He learned the man had no calluses. Smooth hands indicated a white-collar job. Well-manicured nails and the light aftershave affirmed he had money. So did the creak and odor of his leather wallet. The number of bills he rifled through to extract the twenties meant he had a good amount of money.

"Guess you just went to the ATM? Might be good to take some of that cash out of your wallet before you head into the city."

"What?" The odor of fear grew stronger. "How did you know that?" The man waved a hand in front of Benuel's face, no doubt testing to see if he really was blind.

The swish of air he stirred revealed the distance and dimensions of the stranger's movements. Benuel answered the man's unspoken question. "Yes, I'm really blind."

"But—but, how do you know all those things?" Curiosity warred with apprehension in the man's tone.

"I've developed my other senses," Benuel explained, "something most people neglect. They rely too much on sight and miss many other important clues."

"How did you get all the prices right?"

Benuel smiled. "I have my ways." He wasn't about to share his secret, but as he ran his hands over the used items to price them for the shop, he judged quality and flaws. Once he decided on a price, he printed it on the cardboard tag and poked small pinholes into it, so he could tell the cost. From time to time, *Englisch* tourists tried to cheat by telling him the tag had a different price on it. He ignored them and went by touch.

"But you have to ask how much money customers give you and trust they aren't lying to you." The triumph in his voice indicated Benuel's skills intimidated him.

"I can usually tell if they're telling me the truth."

"Yeah, right."

"I'll prove it to you, if you'd like. Open your wallet and hand me any bill in it. You can tell me the truth or lie about the denomination. I'll tell you whether you're being honest."

When the man hesitated, Benuel laughed. "I'm not planning to keep the bills. I'll hand them right back. Also, you need to work on your trust issues. Not everyone's out to cheat you."

"Huh?" The man shifted uneasily in front of the counter, but he drew out his wallet. "Here." He thrust a bill at Benuel. "It's a ten."

"I don't think so." Benuel handed back the money. "Try again."

After six tries, the man conceded. "I guess you do have a sixth sense."

Actually, it had nothing to do with a sixth sense. When people lied, a tiny beat of hesitation preceded the lie, and the timbre of their voices changed slightly due to a tightening of the vocal cords. Both clues were barely perceptible, but Benuel's keen ears detected each nuance. Sometimes a customer's hand shook ever so slightly when giving him a bill of the wrong denomination.

Benuel wasn't about to give away his secrets, so he said, "If someone does fool me, I'll leave that up to God."

"God would let you be cheated?"

No need to see the man's face. The sarcasm in his words made his feelings about God clear. "It seems to me," Benuel said, "you need to get right with God. He'll forgive you for what you've done."

"You don't know the first thing about me." The man snatched up his purchases and hurried to the door. A faint odor of smoke wafted from his clothes. He either rarely smoked or smoked outdoors.

"And one other thing," Benuel called after him just before the door slammed, "You should listen to the person who's been begging you to stop smoking. They're right."

He'd made a guess on that, but evidently he'd guessed right from the strangled curse word that floated through the door just before it slammed. The bells at the top of the door jangled long after the man exited.

"*Daed*," his ten-year-old daughter Susanna scolded as she headed down the steps, "you really need to stop doing that. You'll scare off all our customers."

"Mark my words. That man will be back." Benuel stroked his beard. "God sent him here for a purpose. And he needs to make peace with the Lord."

RYAN STEVENS SAT in his car as the shopkeeper closed down for the night. The man's performance had been amazing. Was he only pretending to be blind? If so, why? How did he know about the smoking? Ryan brought the short sleeve of his shirt close to his nose. No odor he could detect. The nerve-racking part hadn't been the man knowing Ryan was sneaking smokes. Perhaps a slight odor still clung to his clothes. But how did he guess Monica had been haranguing him about it? The whole thing creeped him out.

He'd parked at the far end of the parking lot, but if the shopkeeper truly was blind, he'd never know. When the man emerged, his young daughter held his hand. Ryan ducked so she wouldn't see him sitting in the car. He waited until they'd moved far enough down the path to their house, which was situated behind the building, before he sat up again.

Their backs to him, the man and young girl made their way confidently toward the house. The shopkeeper's step appeared quite steady. Ryan had almost concluded the blindness had been an act when the daughter tightened her grip on her father's arm. He stopped, and she tugged on his sleeve to lead him around a calico cat curled up on the sidewalk. They had no idea Ryan was watching, so the shopkeeper must not have even partial sight, if he couldn't see that large tomcat.

After the two of them disappeared inside the house, Ryan reached into the glove compartment for his last pack of cigarettes. He'd stopped carrying them in his pocket to make it easier to resist temptation. But as he started to tap a cigarette out of the pack, the shopkeeper's words haunted him. Between that and the memory of Monica's sad eyes, guilt overwhelmed him. He tapped the cigarette back into the pack. Then he got out of the car, crossed the parking lot to the dumpster, and tossed in the cigarettes. How could a man he'd just met make such an impact on his life?

The shopkeeper had made him uncomfortable about other things as well. It was almost like he could peer directly into people's souls. The man had gotten a lot of things correct, but he'd made one major mistake. Ryan had no need to ask for forgiveness from a nonexistent God, a God who was only a figment of people's imagination.

CHAPTER 2

*M*ari's twin sister Frannie pulled the horse to a stop at the side of the road. The buggy swayed as it settled into the rutted dirt tracks beside the cornfields. During the whole trip, the summer sun had beaten down on them mercilessly.

"Why are we stopping here?" With the edge of her apron, Mari wiped the sweat beading on her forehead. The nearest farmhouse was only a distant speck on the horizon.

Frannie glanced at the street signs a short distance ahead that marked a deserted country crossroad. "I'm lost."

Her wail woke three-year-old Samuel, who'd been curled on the back seat. He whimpered and rubbed his eyes. Strands of bright orangish-red hair lay plastered to his damp forehead. His straw hat had ended up wedged between his seat and the back of the front seat.

"The last thing I need is for him to start bawling." Frannie rubbed her forehead.

Mari knelt on the seat, so she could reach over and pat her nephew's back to soothe him. He shied away from her touch. Poor boy probably wanted his *mamm* rather than an *aenti* he'd met only two days ago.

When Samuel's eyes locked with hers, he cringed. Mari tried to convey that she wouldn't hurt him as she moved her hand toward him inch by inch. Despite his flinching, she ruffled his damp curls back from his forehead, wishing he had the usual bowl-cut other Amish boys wore. His too-short bangs and almost shaggy sides made him look more like an *Englischer*. Mari had learned not to mention it to her twin sister because she'd explode.

According to Frannie, Samuel had hacked at his hair with scissors when she wasn't looking, so she'd tried to even it out to one length. She kept it covered as best she could with his hat and became furious when he took it off. Mari debated trying to put the hat on him, but with the heat, she let him go without it, hoping Frannie wouldn't notice and berate him.

At the moment, her sister was too upset to pay attention to Samuel or straw hats. Frannie scowled at the small hastily sketched map in her hands. "None of the last three crossroads have shown up on here. And according to the map, we should be heading northwest, but the sun is back there." She pointed to the late afternoon sun behind them. "That would be west, right?"

"I believe so," Mari said. "Could we have missed a turn?"

"No, I didn't miss any turns," Frannie snapped. "The map must be wrong."

"Maybe Ruth only marked the larger intersections."

Frannie glared at her. "Does it look like we'll come to any major roads?"

With fields of ripe corn surrounding them as far as the eye could see and tree-covered mountains on the distant horizon, finding anything but country lanes appeared

8

unlikely. But since childhood, Mari had learned the importance of soothing her sister's temper before it erupted into a major storm.

Seven years in the *Englisch* world had done little to calm Frannie's volatile personality. If anything, she seemed more prone to flying into rages. Mari tried to make allowances for her sister's recent loss. As a widow with a small child, perhaps she channeled her grief into anger rather than tears.

Keep her tone as soft and gentle as possible, Mari offered a suggestion she worried might upset Frannie. "There's a farmhouse up ahead. They might be able to help us find our way."

"How many times do I have to tell you?" Frannie said through gritted teeth. "I don't want to be around people right now. It's much too hard."

"I don't mind going up to the house to ask. You could stay in the buggy and wait."

"I am not stopping at an *Englisch* house."

Her sister wanted to avoid anything *Englisch*. She refused to go into stores or restaurants with cars in the parking lots. Was she trying to avoid temptation now that she'd decided to return to the Amish?

Mari had packed food for the journey, but they'd eaten it earlier, so a drink or snack break would be welcome. And stopping at a farmhouse, even an *Englisch* one, might prevent aimless wandering in the wrong direction.

"Why don't we drive that way to see if we can find an Amish farm?" Mari pointed to the road ahead. Most of the places they'd passed so far had not been promising. Surely with all the large farms ahead, one of them would be Amish.

"What choice do we have?" Bitterness seeped into Frannie's tone. She urged the horse back onto the road and into a trot. She slowed as they neared the farmhouse. "Look at that red truck beside the barn. Definitely not Amish."

Frannie flicked the reins to move the horse past the long, steep driveway.

Mari sighed. She had no problem asking *Englischers* for directions, but she held her tongue. She and Frannie had had this same argument again and again all morning.

They passed several more farms, but Frannie had a reason for not stopping at each one, including an Amish farm where an extended family were having a picnic under a huge oak tree.

Samuel's grizzling turned into full-fledged sobs. The poor boy probably needed to stretch his legs and have a bite to eat. But Frannie's gritted teeth and tight grip on the reins made it clear she had no intention of stopping.

At the next crossroads, a hand-lettered sign for a secondhand shop pointed down a narrow side road. Mari waved toward it. "That might be an Amish shop."

Frannie pulled the horse to a stop and studied the sign. Then she studied the small building in front of a farmhouse. "If that's their parking lot, there's only one buggy in it."

To Mari's relief, her sister turned the horse in that direction.

"Maybe I can get us each some better-fitting clothes." Frannie sounded relieved.

She'd borrowed one of Mari's dresses, but it hung on her too-bony frame, so she'd pinned the apron tightly around her, bunching the dress into folds around her waist. Her nervous energy and fidgeting must be what kept her rail thin.

Poor Samuel had on an old hand-me-down suit of clothes from their youngest brother, who was now grown. If they didn't tilt back the straw hat, it covered Samuel's eyebrows. Mari's heart went out to him. All this must be quite a change for a little boy who'd lived the first three years of his life as an *Englischer*.

Her sister's decision to return to the Amish had been

sudden. Soon after the funeral, she'd packed up Samuel and come straight home, surprising Mari, who'd spent the past five years caring for her aging parents.

Frannie had thrown the household into disarray by insisting Mari accompany her from Lancaster to their *Aenti* Ruth's house in Big Valley. *Mamm*, thrilled about Frannie's return to the faith, encouraged Mari to go along and keep her twin out of trouble. They'd made arrangements for their married siblings to take turns caring for their parents for the rest of the week, and Mari set off with Frannie a day later.

The drive might have been pleasant if Frannie hadn't insisted on driving Mari's buggy. Used to riding in cars, Frannie grew impatient and pushed the horse into a gallop much too often. Mari's requests to slow down, only irritated her sister, who drove faster out of spite.

To Mari's relief, Frannie slowed to a snail's pace going down the narrow lane. Her sister swiveled her head from side to side. She also darted glances in the rearview mirror. Although Frannie had always been edgy and a bit paranoid when they were growing up, those traits seemed to have overtaken her.

Mari wanted to remind her twin that God was caring for them, but she didn't want to risk Frannie's wrath. No doubt, her sister would take Mari's attempt at comfort as criticism.

When they reached the shop, Frannie drove past the marked spaces and parked on a patch of grass among bushes and trees.

"I don't think this is a parking space," Mari ventured. "We should park on the lot."

"I'll park wherever I want." Frannie hopped out and looped the reins around a nearby sapling.

"They have hitching posts." Mari pointed them out, but her sister ignored her.

"Come on," Frannie groused. "What's taking you so long?"

"I thought I'd stay out here with Samuel until he settles down a bit. He's too fussy to take inside just yet."

Frannie hissed out a breath. "Get him in the store now." When Mari hesitated, Frannie huffed. "He needs to get out of the hot sun."

Her sister hadn't worried about that during the hours they'd driven in the broiling heat. She'd ignored Mari's pleas to stop at stores or fast-food places for a brief snack and to cool down. Why was she so insistent on it now? With this being an Amish shop, they'd be lucky to find a battery-powered fan and some open windows.

"Hurry," Frannie urged. She drew in a sharp breath when Mari picked up Samuel. "Where's his hat? Get it on his head right now." She glanced around as if checking that no one had seen him.

Mari didn't blame her. If she were Samuel's *mamm*, she wouldn't want anyone to see his terrible haircut either. She picked up the crying, flailing child, deposited his straw hat on his head, and followed Frannie to the shop.

The bells on the door jingled as they entered, and Samuel stopped crying for a minute as he lifted his head to search for the source of the sound. He pointed to the bells, and in a tear-clogged voice, he called, "Mommm. . ."

"What?" Frannie snapped, and Samuel howled.

The handsome young man behind the counter seemed to be studying them, but his eyes revealed he was blind. He fixed his attention on Frannie, who squirmed. His peaceful and serene expression made Mari regret bringing a screaming child into his store.

She started toward the door. "I'll take him outside a minute until he calms down."

"No!" Frannie shrieked and grabbed her arm. "I don't want him out of my sight."

Though Mari could understand her sister's fear of being parted from her son so soon after losing her husband, she disliked disturbing other customers or the shopkeeper, who stepped from behind the counter and headed toward the squalling.

Mari backed away as he came closer. Would he force her and Samuel out of the store?

"It's all right," he soothed.

Mari was unsure whether his comforting words were directed at her or Samuel, but the kindness in his tone kept her riveted to the spot as he approached. She marveled at how sure his steps were, and when he reached out, his large hand brushed Samuel's forehead without any clumsiness.

The hat tilted back slightly, and Frannie reached over to shove it back in place. The shopkeeper stroked the damp hair protruding from the hat with a gentle finger. Samuel's wails lowered several decibels. Perhaps he needed a man's touch after losing his *daed*.

"Don't touch my son." Frannie reached out to grab the man's arm, but he dropped his hand to his side before she could bat his hand away. Her voice shook as she tried to excuse her rudeness. "He's frightened of strangers."

Mari's cheeks heated at her sister's impoliteness. The shopkeeper had only tried to help, and Samuel hadn't shown any signs of being afraid.

"The poor boy is hot and sweaty," the man said. "Let me get him a drink of water."

"No," Frannie's sharp voice stopped him as he moved toward the counter. "We have water in the buggy. Mari can get it."

Her sister acted as if the man planned to poison Samuel. To be nervous about losing your child after your husband has died was understandable, but Frannie's fears bordered on irrational.

"I'm sorry," Mari apologized to the man, but from his placid expression, he hadn't taken any offense. "You're right about him being thirsty. We should have given him a drink."

"Stop apologizing, Mari, and go get the water," Frannie commanded.

Mari started to the door again, but her sister sucked in a breath.

"Don't take Samuel out there. Give him to me." Frannie reached for her son.

When Mari tried to hand Samuel to her sister, his wails rose even louder and he kicked up such a fuss, Frannie huffed out a breath. "Never mind. I'll go get the water jug myself."

When her sister exited, Mari hesitated to ask a man such a personal question, but being desperate to give Samuel and herself a break, she leaned toward the counter to whisper, "Do you have a bathroom?"

"Of course." The shopkeeper directed her to a small room at the back of the store.

Mari sighed in relief to see running water when she opened the door. After she and Samuel were done, she took a few paper towels and wet them. She wiped her nephew's sweaty forehead before dabbing at her own.

Samuel stopped crying, but his eyes held so much sorrow, Mari wanted to sweep him into her arms and cuddle him close. When she reached for him, though, his eyes rounded in fear, and he backed away.

"I won't hurt you, Samuel," she assured him.

"Not Samuel," he muttered.

Since her sister had arrived two days ago, these were the first words Samuel had spoken. Frannie had decided he should have an Amish name instead of his *Englisch* one, but the poor boy refused to answer when they called him *Samuel*. All these changes so soon after his father's death must be confusing.

His lips set in mutinous lines, he said, "No go."

She wasn't sure of his meaning, but she took a guess. He couldn't understand why they'd left home without his father. "You wish you were back in your old house, don't you?"

Samuel tilted his head to one side, while he studied her warily, but his eyes filled with relief. Mari wished she had a way to erase his heartache. She bent to pull him into her arms, but he backed away.

"You don't want to be held?" she asked. His crying had decreased when she set him on his feet. Perhaps he only wanted to be independent. She reached for his hand.

"Go away," he said, and his eyes filled with tears.

Did he mean he wanted her to go away? Or was he trying to process his father's death? Perhaps trying to tell her his *daed* had gone away? The tears rolling down his cheeks seemed to indicate that.

She squatted to his level. "You miss your *daed*, and don't understand why he went away?"

Samuel's eyes rounded as if surprised she'd understood him. Then he nodded vigorously.

Poor child. Dealing with the suddenness of losing his *daed*, being dragged to a new home where he knew no one, and then traveling for hours to another strange place had to be confusing. Mari tried to reassure him with her eyes as she opened her arms again.

After a brief hesitation, Samuel walked toward her and let her hug him. He protested, a sound deep in his throat, when she tried to lift him into her arms. She continued to hold him close, and when he relaxed a bit, she picked him up. He whimpered but didn't fight her.

A loud screech from the store startled Mari so much, she

almost dropped Samuel. *Oh, no.* Frannie had returned to find them gone. Her poor sister must be frantic.

Samuel tensed in Mari's arms. She opened the door and headed toward the commotion, and Samuel's crying increased the closer they got to the front of the store.

"We're right here," Mari called.

The wildness in Frannie's eyes flickered into anger. "Where were you?"

"We used the bathroom." Mari leaned close to whisper, though she had no idea if her sister could hear her over Samuel's yells.

Her sister glared at her but thrust the large water container and three plastic cups in Mari's direction. "Try giving him a drink. Maybe that will shut him up."

The man's eyebrows rose, drawing Mari's attention to his strong, well-shaped features. He looked to be about thirty, maybe five years older than her and Frannie.

Mari stepped away from Frannie and set Samuel on the floor beside her. Once again, being on his feet decreased his crying. She filled a cup and handed it to him. He gulped down a large sip, and blessed peace reigned.

While he drank, Mari filled a cup and handed it to Frannie. Then she tried to pour one for herself, but barely a half cup dribbled out. Her sister didn't notice, and Mari drained her cup, wishing for more. She wished she'd waited, though, when Samuel held out his empty cup as if asking for more.

Frannie finished hers and handed the cup back. "I'm heading to the bathroom, but I don't want you two to move from here while I'm gone."

As soon as her sister was out of earshot, the shopkeeper stepped from behind the counter. "Let me refill that for you. You didn't get a full cup."

How did he know that? Mari wanted to ask him, but she

held out the container, hoping Frannie would be gone long enough that she wouldn't know.

The man went into a small room behind him and emerged a short while later, holding the full water jug and a homemade fruit and nut bar wrapped in a napkin. "I'm sorry I only have one, but I thought the boy might be hungry." He handed the water container to Mari and then held the bar out to Samuel, who grabbed it and gnawed at it greedily.

"Thank you for your kindness," Mari said. "I know Samuel appreciates it, but he doesn't talk much." In fact, the few short sentences in the bathroom were the first ones she'd heard him speak.

The shopkeeper set a hand on Samuel's shoulder. The small boy lifted his head to look at him. As if sensing this stranger was safe, Samuel gave him a tremulous smile. After two clumsy tries, the man wiped at Samuel's cheeks with a fingertip to dry his tears.

"Would you like a tissue?" he asked Mari as he gently patted Samuel's shoulders and back.

"N-no, thank you." The shopkeeper's closeness had set her pulse galloping. She'd never had such a strange reaction to a man before. Actually, she'd never been this close to any man. He was so near the laundry-fresh smell of his shirt wafted around her, and his arm brushed hers as his fingers moved up and down on Samuel's cheeks.

At Frannie's footsteps clomping toward them on the wooden floorboards, the shopkeeper slipped behind the counter. Samuel shoved the last bite of the bar into his mouth.

"Thank you so much," Mari whispered so her sister couldn't hear. She swallowed hard when a radiant smile lit his face.

"You're welcome, Mari." He kept his voice as low as hers.

She studied him warily. How did he know her name? Oh, of course, Frannie had mentioned it. She was both amazed and a little taken aback. What else had he picked up about them in the short time they'd been here? Not that it mattered. They had nothing to hide, and they'd never see him again.

Frannie grabbed Mari's arm, and she jumped. Samuel opened his mouth to wail, but Mari jiggled him gently.

"It's all right," she soothed, and after a quick glance at her face, he settled for a whine.

Frannie, her jaw set, tugged Mari away from the counter and into the nearest aisle.

CHAPTER 3

he nervous sister's low, desperate whisper reached Benuel's sensitive ears. "Don't tell him where we're going. Just ask for directions to this street." She rattled a paper in her hand. "At least with him being blind, he can't see the map."

The girl she'd called Mari took the paper, headed back to the counter, and said sweetly, "We seem to have gotten lost. On the map, our *aenti* marked this road called Mabry's Mill Road. Have we passed it, or is it up ahead?"

"I didn't pass it," the tense woman muttered.

Benuel stroked his beard. "I don't know what direction you were traveling, but Mabry's Mill Road is about three miles that way." He jerked a thumb over his shoulder. "I suspect you were heading east on the main road." Most likely they'd come from town if they didn't know their way around. He might be wrong about his assumption, but he pointed in that direction.

The other woman sucked in her breath, confirming he'd been correct. "How did he know that?" she whispered.

Perhaps he should have kept that guess to himself so as

not to raise her suspicions. Poor woman seemed to think the world was out to get her or snatch her child from her.

The angry sister might not like his next question, but keeping the poor boy out in this heat wasn't fair. "Can you tell me where you're going? There's likely to be a shortcut from here."

"We're headed to—" The sharp yelp that interrupted Mari's sentence indicated her sister had jabbed her with an elbow.

Why was their destination so secret?

"Never mind," Mari's sister said. "We'll head back in the direction we came from."

"But, Frannie, we—"

Had her sister elbowed her again? Mari stepped sideways, and Benuel hoped she'd moved out of jabbing distance.

So, the other sister's name was Frannie. Her sharp, rapid footfalls were much louder than Mari's, yet he sensed she was thinner. Both sisters seemed to be the same height. "I'd be happy to give you directions to save you the trouble of backtracking."

"No." After a slight rustling from Mari, Frannie followed her crisp response with a grudging, "Thank you."

Benuel hid a smile. Mari must have reminded her sister to use proper manners. He rather hoped she'd elbowed her sister. He liked Mari a lot already, and he'd barely met her. He'd been drawn to her from the moment she'd walked in the door, and foolishly, he'd used his exploration of the small boy's face and shoulders to stay close to her. When he'd accidentally brushed her arm with his, he had to force himself to step back, but slowing the rapid beat of his heart proved impossible. In fact, even the memory of that touch filled him with a longing to be near her again.

He had to concentrate on his customers. From their

barely perceptible movements, they seemed to be having a wordless argument. Mari wanted to get directions, but the nervous tension in Frannie's body spoke of hidden fears. Perhaps she was fleeing an abusive husband and worried about leaving behind clues.

Benuel wished he could assure her he had no intention of betraying her, if that was the case. Instead, he interrupted their silent standoff. "You came in for more than directions though."

At his quiet assertion, Frannie froze. Even Mari pivoted in his direction.

Her sister recovered first. "Yes," she said hesitantly. "I need a few items of clothing. Where are the boys' clothes?"

Benuel pointed to the stairs behind them. "All our clothing is on the second floor."

The three of them trooped up the steps led by the bossy sister. Mari had called her Frannie, but although he shouldn't judge, Benuel couldn't help labeling her other names in his mind.

From each footfall, Benuel assessed their state of mind. Mari, tense and nervous, but trying hard to please, had a slightly heavier tread, indicating she carried the weight of the small boy. The other sister had a sharp, angry press to her strides, but her steps lacked the sureness of Mari's. They contained the jitteriness of a person with an uneasy conscience. Amish marriages were for life, so fleeing from a husband, even an abusive one, could have caused that guilt. Yet, it had an extra apprehensiveness or edginess that troubled him. If Mari had volunteered to help her get away, he hoped she wouldn't get caught in the crosshairs of an angry husband.

The trio did not take long upstairs. They tromped down the steps, again with Frannie in the lead. She laid a pile of garments on the counter, and Benuel set a hand on the stack.

Quite a few outfits for an Amish woman and her son, but it reinforced his impression that she was fleeing. He fingered the tags and swiftly added the total in his head.

After he told her the amount, he reached for bills she held out. As soon as he touched the two crumpled bills, the tremor in her hand made him suspect she intended to cheat him.

"I'm sorry—" he began at the same time as Mari started to speak.

"Frannie, that's not—"

"Hush," Frannie's harsh command ended Mari's protest.

Mari subsided, but her distressed movements in the background convinced him his instinct had been right.

Benuel repeated the total. "Perhaps you didn't hear me correctly?"

Frannie jerked back with the suddenness of a bird flushed from its hiding place, trembling and uncertain of its fate.

"Oh," Mari breathed. "Yes, that must have been the problem." The tension vibrating from her eased.

Benuel was grateful he'd been able to calm her, but a warning flickered in his brain, signaling Frannie's mistake had been deliberate. Like Mari, though, he gave her sister the benefit of the doubt.

This time Frannie handed over the correct amount of money but yanked her hand back when their fingers met. The brief contact revealed one thing. No Amish girl who did chores regularly would have baby soft skin and long fingernails. She couldn't be running from an Amish husband then. An *Englischer*?

With the amount of clothing she'd just purchased, he made a guess. "So, you're coming back to the Amish?"

Frannie recoiled. "Who told you that?"

"No one. It's just an observation I made."

"I see," her voice trembled. "I suppose buying all these clothes. . ."

He opened his mouth to tell her the purchases only confirmed his hunch, but his daughter's caution from yesterday flashed through his mind. He pinched his lips together to stop the flow of words, and instead only nodded as he folded and slid the clothes into a bag. He didn't want to scare away good customers.

Risking Frannie's wrath, he turned toward Mari. "Will you be moving to the area or just visiting?" He hoped she might come around often if they were settling here.

"We're going to our *aenti*'s." Mari took a breath as if preparing to say more.

Frannie's waving arms cut through the air and sent off small shock waves. Mari didn't continue, disappointing Benuel. He'd love to know where to find her and how long she'd be here.

"I hope you'll come again if you're in the area." He handed the bag to Frannie, but directed his words to Mari.

"I'd like that," she said as her sister snatched her purchase from his hands.

After Frannie strode to the door, Mari sidled closer to the counter. "Please forgive Frannie's rudeness. She just lost her husband, so she's overwhelmed with sadness."

"Of course." Benuel had the strangest urge to reach out and caress her hand. He checked the impulse but wished he hadn't after she turned and headed for the open door.

At Frannie's impatient huff, Mari increased her pace.

Benuel wanted to reassure her, so he called after them, using the Amish equivalent of the *Englischer*'s "good luck" phrase, "I wish you all the best. So I do."

Just before the door swung shut behind them, he added, "Don't worry. I won't tell anyone you were here." He hoped those words would calm them and let them know he wouldn't betray them.

Frannie's sharp indrawn breath revealed he'd upset her more than reassured her. The bells barely made a sound as the door closed, so Benuel assumed Mari had shut it.

He sat on the stool behind the counter and propped his head in his hands. He had a lot of work to do—new stock to price, shelves and bins to straighten, furniture to dust—but first he wanted to puzzle out the strange vibrations he'd gotten from the two sisters.

Mari said Frannie's husband had just died. Somehow that didn't ring true. Frannie's body didn't seem to be hunched in on itself, her shoulders weren't weighed down with sorrow. Grieving people usually gave off an aura of loneliness and regret. Often their voices were softer, hesitant, as if unsure of their words. Frannie's voice had been harsh and defensive, not lost and aching.

Perhaps he'd misunderstood Mari's message. His keen ears rarely missed even a whispered word, but perhaps she'd said Frannie had *left* her husband, not *lost* him.

That would fit more with their pattern of behavior. They'd parked their buggy on his lawn, most likely to hide it in the trees. Judging from Frannie's jitteriness and irritability, she had something to hide. And if her husband had died, would she need to buy so many garments? Unless she'd bought black mourning clothes. But the boy wouldn't need to change his clothes. He'd been dressed in rather ill-fitting clothes from the little Benuel had detected by touching the child.

The shop door burst open, setting the bells clanging loudly. Benuel turned a sunny smile toward his daughter.

"You did it again, *Daed*, didn't you?" Susanna let the door slam shut behind her.

"Did what?" Benuel asked innocently, although he

suspected what she meant. She must have been walking down the lane from school and spied the sisters leaving.

"Scared off another customer." The swish of his daughter's dress told him she'd put her hands on her hips.

"I wasn't trying to." Benuel sighed. He just couldn't resist asking questions or making comments to confirm his theories. He hoped he hadn't scared off Mari. Although if she planned to visit her aunt, what would she need in a secondhand shop?

Susanna expelled a long, exasperated breath. "That one twin looked really upset."

"Twins, eh?"

"Yes, they were twins. They looked so much alike, it'd be hard to tell them apart."

Not for Benuel. He could do that in an instant. "Hmm... They were the same height, but one seemed much skinnier than the other."

"She was. Too thin. She looked like she hadn't eaten a proper meal in a long time. But their faces were identical."

Benuel suspected eating had little to do with Frannie's thinness. Fidgety people often burned a lot of calories. If she'd truly lost her husband, perhaps she worried about her little boy. Caring for a child without a spouse was a major concern. He should know.

Before he could plunge into sorrow over the past, Susanna hurried toward the counter. "What do you want me to do first?"

"If you could record this morning's sales in the ledger, that would be a help."

His daughter stopped abruptly. "You were right. That man from yesterday is getting out of his car. He did come back. How did you know?"

"He forgot to buy shoes." From the way the man's shoes had clomped a slight extra beat each time he took a step,

Benuel suspected he'd been wearing slip-on shoes, perhaps loafers. "I had a hunch he might realize his shoes didn't match the rest of his outfit."

Susanna giggled. "Yes, he does look funny. But it's not only his shoes. He's dressed in our clothes, but he doesn't look Amish. Why is he pretending to be something he's not?"

Benuel had wondered the same thing. When the door opened, he faced that way to greet the man with a smile. "Hello, again. I thought you might be back. If you're looking for shoes, they're upstairs in the bins along the far wall."

"H-how did you know what I came in for?"

With a shrug, Benuel answered, "Just guessed." He wished he could deduce the answers to the rest of his questions as easily.

A CHILL RAN down Ryan's spine when the shopkeeper greeted him and directed him to the right spot. This was almost spooky.

He clumped upstairs to the shoe bins. Before he left Lancaster, he should have thought to grab a pair of his black lace-up shoes to replace his well-polished loafers. Brown slip-on shoes looked ridiculous with this Amish get-up he was wearing. And city-slicker shoes would give him away. Ryan dug through the bins of men's shoes, hoping to unearth a tag for his size. He laughed at himself for thinking the Amish wore special shoes. They were similar to a pair of black lace-up shoes in his closet at home. He snatched the first pair in his size. He started toward the stairs, but then stopped.

What if Amish shoes weren't a standard size? He'd better try them on to be sure. Ryan propped himself up with one hand and removed his loafer. He slipped on one shoe, and to his relief, it fit. He took it off and did the same with the other. He'd never purchased used shoes before, but these well-worn ones seemed like they'd be comfortable. No breaking in needed.

As he headed downstairs, the man who'd waited on him yesterday stood behind the counter smiling in his direction. "Found what you needed?"

"Yes." The uncanny way this man seemed to ferret out information made Ryan majorly nervous. He'd almost avoided coming in here again today. Originally, they'd chosen this place because it was off the beaten path and the owner wouldn't be able to identify him later. Now he worried he'd made a major mistake.

"I figured you'd be back," the shopkeeper said. "By the way, my name's Benuel. Benuel King. Since you're aiming to be part of this community, I suppose we should introduce ourselves."

Ryan stopped dead partway down. *How does he know my plans?* "What made you think I'd be back?" His words sounded a bit defensive, but the man—Benuel, he'd said his name was—had caught him off guard again.

Benuel chuckled. "Pretty simple really. You forgot to get shoes. Glad you found a pair that fit."

Ryan's fingers tightened on the pair of shoes in his hand. *How did he guess I picked out shoes? I could be walking down here emptyhanded.* Ryan descended the rest of the stairs and set the shoes on the counter.

"Good choice," Benuel said, cradling a shoe in one hand while the fingers of his other hand slid along the string to the cardboard price tag. "And it was a wise idea to try them on. Shoes from this company sometimes run a little small."

So Benuel had been listening. *But how did he hear me trying them on? I was quiet. And how does he know who manufactured those shoes? Can he tell that by feeling them?* Ryan could use someone like Benuel on his side. Although, once again, the thought ran through his mind that the man was faking his blindness. But the cat yesterday disproved that.

"That'll be eight dollars," Benuel said.

Ryan decided to test him. He'd emptied out his wallet yesterday after Benuel's warning, so he had only a few bills in it. He held out a five. "Here's a ten."

Benuel reached for it, and Ryan couldn't help chuckling to himself when the shopkeeper slid it into the drawer. He'd fooled him.

When Benuel stood there unmoving, Ryan demanded, "Where's my change?"

The shopkeeper reached in the drawer and withdrew two one-dollar bills, and Ryan couldn't wait to crow over his mistake. He'd give the man the right change. He hadn't intended to cheat Benuel, only prove a point.

But Benuel didn't hand over the change.

"Can I have my money?" Ryan hoped his gloating wasn't obvious in his voice. He reached across the counter, eager to snatch the money from Benuel's hand and point out his error.

"Certainly," Benuel said, "as soon as you give me the rest of the payment."

Ryan's mouth hung open. Sheepishly, he reached into his wallet and handed over another five. "I wasn't really planning to cheat you."

"I could tell," Benuel's tone remained as placid as his face. "You have a need to test people. If I can give you a piece of advice, learning to trust others—and God—will change your life."

Ouch! That zinger hit right where Monica had stabbed him in their last argument. Being around this Amish man unnerved him.

As Benuel slid the shoes into a recycled paper bag, a young girl emerged from the back room and went to stand beside her *daed*. At least he assumed Benuel was her *daed*. They both had the same brown hair with reddish tints and green eyes.

The girl studied Ryan closely with her head cocked to one side as if examining him for flaws. Between her scrutiny and her father's uncanny ability to read people, the two of them might as well be inspecting him under a microscope.

"So. . .what brings you to this area?" Benuel asked as he lifted the bag. He didn't extend it across the counter, but stood still, as if waiting for an answer.

"I have a new insurance territory." As soon as he said the words, Ryan wished he could take them back. That had been his cover when he traveled down here, but now that he was walking around dressed in Amish clothing, he needed to change his story.

He hadn't expected to be challenged by a shopkeeper before he established his new identity. "I mean, I used to sell insurance, but now I, um, sell feed. . . You know, like for cattle and horses. I work for a distributor. They gave me this Amish territory, so I thought if I dressed the part. . ." That sounded so lame.

"I see." Benuel kept a poker face as handed over the bag. "Don't worry. I'm good at keeping secrets."

Ryan cringed. He'd blown it. So much for going undercover.

CHAPTER 4

$\mathcal{B}$enuel once again let his fingers brush the stranger's as the man took the bag, trying to sense more beyond what the man had said. Selling insurance fit with the smooth hands and money. That might be his real job, but Benuel had to choke back laughter at that answer.

He'd almost blurted out, *You're hoping to sell insurance to the Amish? I don't think dressing in Amish clothes will help. Or driving car while masquerading as an Amish man.*

At least the man had sense enough to know the Amish didn't buy insurance, and he'd changed his story rather quickly. But even his new excuse rang hollow. If he felt the need to clarify what "feed" is to people who used horses every day, he wouldn't get far. But why would he think dressing Amish would help him sell anything?

In some ways that story seemed even more fishy than his first one. Although the Amish preferred doing business with members of their own community, they were more than willing to buy from *Englischers*. Benuel had his doubts, though, that many of his friends would make agreements with a fake Amish man who spoke with a Jersey accent.

Benuel was still pondering this as the man strode to the door. Just before he exited, the man stopped.

"By the way," he asked in a casual tone, "did you happen to see— Oops, I mean—"

Benuel wished people wouldn't get so upset about using the word *see* around him. There were many different kinds of sight.

The man stumbled on, "Did two Amish women come in here with a small boy?"

Beside Benuel, Susanna started to answer, but he signaled her under the counter to stay silent.

"We have many Amish customers with children. But why would you be looking for Amish women? You should be aware you can't court an Amish woman unless you belong to the church. Were you planning to do that?"

The man's silence showed he'd been taken aback by the question. "No, no, nothing like that. Someone mentioned seeing them come in here earlier. I, um, had something I needed to ask them."

Alarm bells went off in Benuel's brain. Earlier he'd wondered if Frannie had been escaping from an abusive husband. And he'd suspected she'd been married to an *Englisher*. Her son's odd haircut and too-big hat made Benuel curious. Had they recently returned to the Amish, or was she pretending to be Amish to escape from a dangerous domestic situation? This man didn't give off the vibes of a stalker, but sometimes the quieter ones fooled you.

"So did you see them?" the man persisted.

"Who?" Benuel hoped he sounded innocent. He didn't want to put Frannie—or Mari—in danger.

"So, they were in here."

The certainty in the man's voice grated on Benuel. "I never said any such thing."

31

"You didn't have to. The way you're evading my questions gave me the answer. Now which way did they go?"

Benuel only smiled. "Remember I told you I'm good at keeping secrets?"

WITH A HUFF, Ryan let the door slam shut behind him. He'd not only blown his cover, he'd revealed his interest the women he was tailing. He couldn't believe he'd made such an amateur mistake. If only he could enlist Benuel's help in his search. He had an odd suspicion the shopkeeper would be able to find Frannie.

Although Benuel refused to divulge any information, he'd given Ryan his first concrete clue. Frannie had stopped here. Likely she'd done the same thing he had and purchased clothing. The people he'd talked to who had spotted them traveling this way indicated she was dressed in Amish clothing, probably borrowed from her sister.

The fact that they were twins made his hunt much easier. Many people were surprised to see Amish twins who were a mirror image of each other, so they remembered the sisters. Most had not seen a small boy with them, but with as young as he was, the buggy sides could have hidden him from view.

He had to find them before Frannie harmed the boy.

AFTER THEY'D LEFT Benuel's shop, Frannie backtracked to Mabry's Mill Road. By the time they reached *Aenti* Ruth's house, the intense heat had plastered Mari's damp dress to her back. Poor Samuel's hair was drenched with sweat because Frannie insisted he put on the new straw hat and keep it on.

Samuel had stopped whimpering, but he fixed Mari with such pleading eyes that she longed to hold him on her lap and cuddle him. The minute she suggested it, though, Frannie snapped.

"Absolutely not. He needs to stay in the back."

The finality of her sister's response made Mari's heart ache for poor Samuel. She almost sang with gratitude when they finally turned into their *aenti's* driveway.

Ruth had her windows open and a small battery-powered fan that created a slight breeze, but Mari couldn't wait until the sun went down and the day cooled off. She offered to help her *aenti* with chores, while Frannie went upstairs to rest.

After a light supper, they all retired early. Bone-deep weary, Mari fell into bed and drifted off to sleep as soon as she closed her eyes.

A tug on her sheet startled her awake in the middle of the night.

His eyes wide with fear, Samuel stood beside her bed. She held out her arms. He tilted his head as if deciding whether he could trust her. Then he pattered over and let her lift him onto the bed. Cuddling him close, she murmured soothing sounds.

Tears ran down his cheeks, and she brushed them away with a gentle finger. "You missing your *daed*?"

His head bobbed up and down, and she hugged him even tighter. Poor little one. Mari prayed God would ease his pain, then she hummed hymns from the *Ausbund* until he fell asleep.

She woke before the sun rose to do her chores. Her mind still fuzzy from sleep, she struggled figure out where she was and why small feet kept kicking her back. The room came into focus. Ruth's house. Mari rolled over to find Samuel frowning and pummeling the air with his fists in his sleep. He looked as if he were fighting someone or something. She gathered him into her arms and stroked the hair back from his forehead.

He snuggled closer and sighed. "Mom," he whispered. Then his eyes popped open, and he stared up at her. Fear flashed in his eyes, and he struggled to get away.

"It's all right. I'm your *Aenti* Mari."

Samuel's face relaxed, but her worry increased. The small boy seemed frightened of his mother. On the trip here, Mari had witnessed Frannie's harshness toward him, and she recalled her sister's meanness during their childhood. Mari hoped Frannie wasn't mistreating Samuel, but she feared the worst.

Her sister was still asleep, so Mari helped Samuel dress in one of the outfits they'd purchased yesterday. He *rutsched* around, clearly not used to these clothes, but he didn't protest. Then he took her hand, and they went downstairs together.

After Mari fed him a slice of bread with apple butter, he followed her around, clinging to her skirt and glancing around with anxiety. She took him outside to feed the chickens and horses. He backed away when the chickens swarmed toward them, pecking at the food Mari scattered. She tried to encourage him to pour water into the large hanging container in the chicken coop and gather eggs in the basket, but Samuel only watched her warily from a safe distance. And he flattened himself against the barn door while she fed the horses. The pony nickered, and Samuel bawled.

Mari knelt in front of him and took him into her arms. He sobbed as if his heart were broken. The poor boy missed his father. After she'd calmed him, Mari lifted him into her arms and carried him to the pony's stall. When the pony stuck its head over the half-door, she encouraged him to pet it.

"Soft," he whispered.

Maybe the horses would work their usual spell, making the boy's adjustment easier. She'd make sure he had horse time every day. Perhaps she'd even be able to teach him to ride, depending on how long Frannie planned to stay.

Ruth had insisted they could remain as long as they liked. Mari enjoyed being here in Big Valley surrounded by mountains. Samuel seemed more relaxed here too.

A shrill scream from inside the house startled both Mari and Samuel. Mari hurried from the barn with him in her arms.

Frannie's crying stopped when Mari entered the kitchen. "What were you doing? I told you I didn't want him outside."

After they'd arrived yesterday, Frannie had insisted Samuel must stay inside at all times. She claimed the sun made him ill.

That made no sense at all. If it were true, why did she let him get so hot in the buggy? Granted, the sunlight came in through the front windows and wouldn't be as strong when he was in the back seat. But Mari kept her protests to herself. She didn't want to stir up trouble.

No child should be cooped inside all day, and as far as Mari could tell, Samuel had experienced no harmful effects from his brief time outside. Granted, the sun had barely risen. Still, his sadness might lift a little with some outdoor playtime. With a sigh, she bustled around the kitchen helping her *aenti* fix breakfast.

When they sat at the table, Mari bowed her head for the silent prayer. Across the table forks clattered, and her eyes flew open. Frannie and Samuel had begun eating. Mari stared at her sister in shock. Samuel had been raised *Englisch*, so his mistake was understandable, but her sister—?

When Ruth opened her eyes to gaze at her, Frannie huffed out a breath and set down the bite she'd been about to eat. Then she reached out and forced Samuel's spoon back down to his plate. He looked up with startled eyes.

Before he started to cry, Mari explained, "We always pray before we eat." She took his hands and set them in his lap, saying, "Paddies down." She'd keep his hands covered so he didn't move them while they prayed. How sad to have to do this with a three-year-old. Families with very young children taught them this, but if Samuel hadn't learned this, he likely didn't know how to say 'The Lord's Prayer' either." She'd need to teach him the words.

Samuel's forehead wrinkled, but he obeyed. Mari's heart ached for him. Had her sister taught him nothing about God? She'd begin remedying that right away.

Frannie flounced off upstairs after the meal, likely to avoid the dishes and the lessons on God and prayer. While they cleaned up together, Ruth and Mari included Samuel, letting him help with chores while they took turns telling him about God and teaching him the words to "The Lord's Prayer." They told him why they said the prayer and explained what each line meant. Samuel soaked up all the lessons, and Mari thanked the Lord that the small boy had such an open heart and eager spirit to learn about God.

When they finished the household jobs, Mari settled Samuel on the living room floor with a Bible story book and a few small wooden toys they'd played with in childhood. She wished Frannie had saved a few of Samuel's toys from home, so he'd have some familiar things. Every time she mentioned things like that, Frannie went into hysterics. She didn't want to remind her sister of all she'd lost. Frannie said they'd had to sell everything to pay for their train tickets home. That, on top of losing her husband, must have been awful.

"I'm going to muck out the horses' stalls," Mari said after her *aenti* settled in a chair by the window with some mending. At home, *daed* insisted on them doing that chore every morning, but Ruth appeared a bit too frail to handle all the work.

"Bless you, Mari." Ruth looked up from threading her needle. "One of the neighbor boys comes over a few times a week to help, but I wish it could be done every day."

"I'll see to it every day while we're here." Mari hoped they'd stay a long time, because being here brought her such peacefulness.

As soon as the "feed" salesman departed, Benuel told his daughter to watch out the window until the man pulled out of the parking lot.

"He's gone now, *Daed*. What are you planning to do?"

Benuel wasn't sure, but he had to find Mari and warn her and her sister a man was looking for them. The only clue he had to their whereabouts was Mabry Mill Road. He'd head there to see what he could find out.

"Let's close early today and hook up the buggy."

"Why?" Susanna stepped behind the counter and gently elbowed him out of the way, so she could open the cash drawer. She counted and bundled the bills while Benuel slid coins into sleeves that they placed in the zippered money pouch he took to the bank every few days.

"I'm worried about those twins who were in here earlier. That man seems to be following them. I should at least warn them."

"You know where they went?"

"No, but we need to find out."

"They turned right when they left the parking lot." Susanna slid the stacks of bills into the pouch. "Shall I put up the closed sign and shut the blinds?"

"*Danke*. Could you also run in and make us some sandwiches? I have no idea how long it will take. I'll lock the store and hitch up the horse."

By the time Susanna returned, Benuel had the buggy ready to go. His daughter hopped up and took the reins, and he climbed into the passenger side. "Let's head to Mabry Mill Road."

A short while later, Susanna made the final turn. "What now?" she asked.

"I guess we just stop at every farmhouse to see if anyone has seen the twins."

"Do you want me to go up and ask?"

Benuel nodded. "That would be the quickest way."

Susanna pulled into the first driveway and stopped. Then she handed the reins to him. "I'll be right back." She returned with discouraging news.

They moved down the street, stopping at each house. No one had seen the twins. Benuel disliked making his daughter run to each door, but if he went, he'd need her help negotiating the walkways, steps, and porches. Assisting him would only slow her down, not decrease the number of steps she took.

Each time Susanna hurried off, Benuel prayed for God's protection over Mari, Samuel, and Frannie. After none of Susanna's stops proved fruitful, Benuel grew discouraged. Suppose the twins hadn't turned down this road after all. Frannie had been cagey about where they were going. Maybe she'd named a nearby road to throw him off.

"Do you want to keep going?" Susanna asked after she

returned with another *no* answer. "No one seems to have seen them."

"Let's try a few more houses." He couldn't give up yet. Suppose the fake Amish man found them first? Would he do them harm? That thought spurred him to keep moving. "I wish I could take your place, *dochder*."

"I don't mind." Susanna assured him. "Besides it's important to help people when they're in trouble."

"*Jah*, it is." He tamped down his guilt. Part of his motivation was to see Mari again.

Two houses later, Susanna stopped the buggy. "There's a small stand selling green beans, corn, and tomatoes. I'll ask the little boy and girl."

After a short time, Susanna bounced into the wagon and, with a lilt in her voice, informed him, "They turned left at the next crossroad."

"Good work," Benuel told her. "I hope someone saw them on that road."

Once she'd turned the corner, Susanna flicked the reins, and the horse broke into a trot.

Benuel grabbed the edge of the seat. "Whoa! We don't want to have an accident."

"The Fisher girls up ahead are closing up their roadside stand. I'm trying to catch them before they go inside."

"Great." His daughter had been a big help in this search. *Please, Lord, help us to find the twins*, Benuel prayed as Susanna leaped out to talk to her two friends from church. It seemed they'd traveled in a huge circle. Too bad Frannie hadn't given him the address where they were headed. He could have given them a shortcut.

Susanna soon brought the Fisher girls over to talk to him. "They have the information you need, *daed*."

"We saw the twin ladies," the older Fisher girl said.

Benuel identified her by her rich, bell-like tones. The

younger girl had a squeakier voice. "Which way did they go?" he asked.

"We didn't see because we had several customers to take care of, but Ruth Flaud visited *Mamm* yesterday and mentioned her twin nieces would be coming to visit today."

That certainly fit. Mari said they'd be visiting their *aenti*. "*Danke*. We'll pay this Ruth a visit."

Humming a tune from the *Ausbund*, Susanna climbed into the buggy. "We did it. I got directions to the house."

"Almost," Benuel cautioned. "We haven't found them yet. But I appreciate all your efforts to gather information." As long as Mari and her sister hadn't paid a brief visit, he hoped they'd still be there.

CHAPTER 5

*M*ari found many jobs to do inside all day, so she postponed the mucking. Ruth's arthritis had been bothering her for months, so she hadn't been able to clean as well as usual. Mari washed all the windows with vinegar and shined them with newspaper, then scrubbed all the floors on her hands and knees to get into all the cracks and crevices. After scouring the propane oven and refrigerator, she helped Ruth prepare supper.

Meanwhile Frannie had holed up in her room. She spent most of the day sleeping, except when she called in a grumpy voice for Mari to bring her a glass of water or something to eat. She didn't even come down for meals.

Ruth's face crumpled into lines of distress. "Is Frannie ill?" she asked after Mari's fifth trip up the stairs.

"*Neh*, she's eating everything. I expect it's grief. She only recently lost her husband."

"I lost my husband when my daughters were young, and I never stayed abed. Too little work and too much self-pity isn't good for a body."

Mari agreed, but without Frannie, Samuel had begun

blossoming. He said a few words here and there, and he followed Mari around like a baby chick.

As dusk settled over the mountains and fields, Mari finally headed out to muck the stalls. The screen door banged open behind her, and she turned. Samuel stood on the back porch.

"Would you like to see the horses again?" she asked.

He nodded shyly.

Surely Frannie wouldn't object. The sun sat low on the horizon. No danger there. Mari waited for him to cross the lawn, then she held out her hand for him to hold. To her surprise, he slid his hand into hers. Warmth wrapped around her heart. Taking care of her parents for the past six years had meant no courting. She'd missed out on marriage and children, and now it was too late. But having a nephew might allow her some of that joy.

Samuel held his nose as Mari forked out the soiled straw. When she laid down fresh straw, though, Samuel worked with her. After they finished, she held him up so he could pet the horses. He ran a hand down Button's silky muzzle, and his whole face brightened with the first genuine smile she'd seen in the past two days.

Hand in hand, they exited the barn. A young girl raced toward them. "My *daed* wants to talk to you."

Had Ruth come out to the barn? Mari glanced over her shoulder, expecting her *aenti* to be standing behind her. It took a moment to sink in. The girl meant her. Who was her *daed*? And why would a stranger want to talk to her?

"Please will you come with me? He's out in the buggy."

Mari reached down for Samuel and swung him into her arms, so she could follow the girl's rapid steps. Just before she reached the buggy, she stopped short. The shopkeeper sat inside.

"Hello," he said, "I don't know if you remember me, but I'm Benuel King. You were at my shop earlier today."

How could she ever forget? His deep voice struck a chord in Mari that set bells chiming. For one heavenly moment, her spirit took wings. Had he come to see her?

"H-how did you find me?"

Benuel put an arm around the young girl who'd climbed into the driver's seat of the buggy. "My daughter persisted in asking all the neighbors until we found a few with some answers."

His daughter? Her spirit, soaring only moments before, plunged like a diving bird. Of course, he had a family. She'd ignored his beard this morning when he stood near her in the shop, but she had no right to do that. His beard, shining with auburn threads in the dying sunlight, proved he belonged to another woman. Why had she allowed herself this forbidden fantasy?

"I'd better take Samuel into the house. He should have a bath." And so should she. She hoped she was standing downwind of him. *What does it matter?*

"I understand," Benuel said. "I'll only take a minute or so of your time."

He'd come all the way out here, only to leave so soon? Mari tried not to let her disappointment show.

"I wouldn't have bothered you, but after you and your sister left, a man came in the store and asked if I'd seen Amish twins accompanied by a small boy. I assume he meant you three."

It certainly sounded like it. But who would be looking for them? Her brothers would go to a neighbor's phone shanty and call rather than driving all this way. *Daed* was in no shape to travel. "Did the man give his name?"

Benuel shook his head. "I learned little about him, except he's an *Englischer* who's now dressing in Plain clothes."

43

"Whatever for?"

"I couldn't figure it out." He took a deep breath. "I know it's not my business, but I wondered if your sister was fleeing from an abusive relationship."

What? Maybe Benuel hadn't heard her explanation when they were in the store. Mari shook her head but realized he couldn't see it. "No, Frannie's husband died recently, and she returned home to the Amish."

BENUEL TRIED to piece together the story. So, he hadn't misunderstood Mari earlier. She'd said Frannie "lost" her husband. Benuel wanted to confirm his hunch. "She was married to an *Englischer*?"

"Yes, for seven years."

The sadness in Mari's voice tugged at his heart. She really cared for her sister. Benuel wished he had some way to comfort her. He longed to reach out and touch her, but that wouldn't be appropriate. He tried to convey his sympathy in words. "That must have been hard."

"It was. I'm so glad she's back."

"I am too." For Mari's sake. And for Frannie's too, of course. "But who would be looking for you? And what would he want?"

"I expect Frannie would know. Perhaps it's one of her relatives hoping to see Samuel?"

Benuel puzzled over her response. "If it's a relative, why does he need to disguise himself? Surely Frannie would welcome her son's family, wouldn't she?"

"I would think so." Yet Mari's voice wavered slightly, as if she wanted to believe in her sister, but loyalty warred with uncertainty.

Before he could question her further, Frannie's screech carried through the open window. "Mari!"

"Oh, no!" Mari jumped to her feet and reached for Samuel's hand. "I'm sorry, but we need to go. I'll tell Frannie what you said." She rushed toward the house but turned to call over her shoulder, "Thank you for coming out here to tell us."

The back door banged open. "Where's Samuel?" High-pitched tension vibrated in Frannie's voice. "What did I say about taking him outside?"

"The sun is on the horizon." Mari's soft, placating tone did little to soothe her sister.

Frannie spat out each word. "Get him in here now."

Her command raised Benuel's hackles. He didn't like the way she ordered Mari around. It really wasn't his place to interfere, but he cleared his throat. Frannie's sharp indrawn breath told him she'd just noticed his presence.

"What's he doing here?" she muttered.

Although she'd moved far away, Mari's answer floated to him. "He came to bring us some news."

"That man knows nothing about us." Frannie was dismissive, but then her voice shook with fear. "But how did he know where to find us?"

"I didn't ask."

"He faked his blindness." Frannie's tone rose sharp and shrill. "He looked at the map."

Perhaps he should slip away now. He'd delivered the message he needed to bring. He'd worried they might be in danger, but maybe he'd been mistaken. He'd read Mari's vibes and listened carefully to her tone. She hadn't panicked when she heard his news. And her sister was a recent widow, so the story he'd concocted about a vengeful ex trying to harm Frannie had been totally wrong.

Benuel motioned for his daughter to head for their

buggy. Susanna took his arm and helped him over the uneven ground.

Behind them, Frannie had gone into a long diatribe about him being a possible kidnapper. And how you could never trust strangers.

Benuel sighed. How hard it must be to go through life always anticipating others would hurt you. And he could only imagine what it was like for poor Mari, who seemed so open and trusting, to live with her.

MARI CRINGED, wishing Frannie would speak softly. Benuel had gone out of his way to be kind only to be accused of terrible deeds.

She reached out and took her sister's arm, hoping to pull her into the house as rapidly as possible, but Frannie shook her off.

"I can't believe you took a chance like that," Frannie practically shrieked. "What if something happened to Samuel?"

Mari opened the door to usher her sister inside, but she couldn't resist peeking over her shoulder. Benuel's daughter was leading him toward the buggy. Mari hoped he was far enough away that he couldn't hear her sister's unkindness. She needed to get him off her mind.

Frannie's rant continued after they entered the kitchen. When the screen door slammed shut behind them, Frannie turned and latched it. Then she whirled to face Mari.

Her face red, Frannie's words shot out like bullets, hitting Mari right in the heart. "You are never to take Samuel out of the house again. Ever. You can't be trusted."

Mari longed to protest, to defend herself. But as angry as her sister was right now, Frannie wouldn't hear Mari's explanation. Maybe she should wait to tell Frannie about Benuel's message. If Frannie didn't trust her own sister with Samuel, for sure and certain Frannie would never want her husband's relatives around her son.

After Frannie bathed Samuel and took him upstairs to put him in bed, Mari sank into a chair at the kitchen table and mulled over what Benuel had said. The only sticking point seemed to be the man choosing to dress Amish. Why would an *Englischer* do that?

The only reason Mari could come up with was that this relative knew of Frannie's refusal to go near any *Englischers*. Did he think pretending to be Amish would allow him to spend time with Samuel?

Many *Englischers* didn't realize how difficult it was to turn Amish. Some thought they could live without electricity and cars, wear Plain clothes, and do farm chores. They had no idea they'd need to spend years learning the *Deutsch* language, and they'd have to study the *Dordrecht Confession* and attend baptismal classes.

She doubted this man intended to do all that, but he likely had no idea that dressing Plain wouldn't fool Frannie, who'd grown up Amish. She'd immediately spot him as a fake. Even Benuel, who couldn't see the man, had pegged him as an imposter.

What Mari couldn't figure out is why he'd plan such an elaborate ruse when Frannie most likely would recognize his face, Plain clothes or not. Unless he thought looking Amish might get him close enough to plead with Frannie. If he dressed *Englisch*, she'd probably run or hide.

Darkness fell, but Mari still sat at the table. Now, though, she daydreamed about the shopkeeper. He'd been so nice and caring. He'd been so gentle even Samuel had warmed up to him. So had she, perhaps more than she should have. And her heart had leaped when she'd spied him outside.

How kind he'd been to come all this way just to tell them someone was looking for them. He'd misunderstood what she'd told him about Frannie's husband when they were in the shop, so he'd worried they were in danger.

If she ever had a chance to court, she'd want to find someone like Benuel. Someone tender and protective, who put others needs first. If only. . .

Mari jumped when Ruth set a hand on her shoulder.

"I'm sorry," Ruth said. "I didn't mean to frighten you."

Pressing her hands over her rapidly beating heart, Mari sucked in a breath. "It's all right."

Ruth gently squeezed Mari's shoulder. "I came down to let you know Frannie and Samuel are asleep, and I'm headed off to bed. Did you want me to turn on the propane lamp? I don't like to think of you sitting here in the dark."

Mari slid back her chair and stood. "I'll head up with you. It's time for me to be in bed." Dawn would be here soon, and she had plenty of chores to do.

"Thank you for all the help you gave me today." Ruth padded toward the stairs, and Mari followed.

"I'm happy to help. I know it's not easy having three extra visitors."

"You're not visitors; you're family. I enjoy having company. It can be lonely being here by myself."

"And we love being here with you." At least Mari did. She probably shouldn't speak for her sister. These days she was unsure how Frannie felt about anything—except irritated and angry. Underneath all that, though, her sister was dealing with grief. They needed to give her time to recover.

CHAPTER 6

*R*yan pulled his car in front of the darkened house and reached in the glove compartment for a cigarette. He gritted his teeth and clenched his fists. He'd forgotten he'd thrown out his last pack. Right now, he regretted it. His hands were jittery, and he needed to calm his nerves.

It would be a long night, but he was pretty sure he'd found the right place. Now all he could do was wait to see. He leaned his seat back and closed his eyes. He couldn't afford to oversleep because the family would rise early. He needed to be alert to catch them by surprise.

To be on the safe side, he set the alarm on his phone for four-thirty. He'd move his car elsewhere then, so it wouldn't be noticeable, and approach the house on foot. Meanwhile, he'd get some rest.

MARI ROSE at dawn to do the milking. She tiptoed past Frannie and Samuel's door so she didn't wake them and headed down the stairs. She'd just pulled on her coat when a door upstairs creaked. She waited for a moment, but hearing nothing more, she assumed it was her imagination and headed out the back door.

When she was partway to the barn, the back door opened. Mari whirled around in time to spy a small figure easing the door shut. She drew in a breath. What was Samuel doing out here so early in the morning?

He didn't look in her direction. Instead of heading toward her and the barn, he slipped along the side of the house. Where was he going?

Mari hurried toward him. "What are you doing?" she whispered.

Samuel stopped in his tracks, and he looked up at her with wide fearful eyes. "Go home," he said.

Her eyes filled with tears. The poor boy. He didn't understand his *daed* was gone. She knelt and pulled him into her arms. How could she explain he'd never be going back his home and he'd never see his father again? She ached for the small boy. All she could do was wrap her arms around him and hold him close while he sobbed.

After his tears were spent, he lay in her arms, limp and exhausted. Mari couldn't take him back into the house while she did chores. He might escape and try to get home. If her sister were less prickly, Mari would wake Frannie to let her know, but with her sister's recent loss and her volatile temper, it would be better to let her sleep.

"Let's go to the barn." Mari struggled to her feet, still holding Samuel, who remained listless until they entered the barn. She took him over to Button and was relieved when Samuel ran his hand over the horse's muzzle.

"Would you like to help me feed her?"

When he nodded, she set him on his feet, took his hand, and led him over to the pile of hay. She demonstrated picking up one square bale and putting it in the wire hay rack outside the stall. Then she handed Samuel a bale. He wrapped his arms around it and carried it to the next stall. He toddled back and forth to feed the third horse. His eyes lit up when she let him scoop grain into each feed box.

Then she led him in to feed the two cows. He watched fascinated while she milked the first one. She let him help with the next more docile cow. With her help, he squirted a small stream of milk and laughed as it pinged into the bucket.

Mari couldn't help smiling at his delight. His smiles were few and far between. She finished the milking with Samuel leaning against her, watching intently. Then hand in hand, they exited the barn with the pail.

A man materialized out of the damp gray mist, and Mari jumped back. Her first instinct was to conceal Samuel from view. She shielded him behind her body and set the bucket on the ground.

"Can I help you?" Mari tried to keep the nervousness from her voice, but her throat had tightened.

"Is that your son?" The man tried to peer behind her.

"N-no." So much for trying to appear calm. Something about this man seemed off. At first glance, he appeared Amish, a closer look revealed many oddities. No hair showed under his straw hat. He should have a bowl cut, unless he was bald. The minute he spoke, though, his speech betrayed him.

This must be the man Benuel had warned her about. If he was one of Samuel's relatives, she should be friendly and welcoming. She attempted a smile. "Are you the one who was asking about us in the secondhand shop?"

The man took a step back, his eyes wide. "How did you know that? Did Benuel call you?"

Mari laughed. "We don't have a phone, so no, he didn't call."

Muttering something about ESP, the man stepped closer and tried to move around her.

She turned slightly to hide Samuel from the intensity of his gaze. When he couldn't see Samuel, he turned the searchlight of his eyes on her. "So the boy isn't yours?"

Was it her imagination, or did it sound as if he planned to snatch Samuel? Any relative would be curious about the boy's wellbeing, but his inflection and the judgment in his eyes suggested she had no right to this child.

Did the relatives want to raise Samuel? Maybe they didn't want him raised Amish? Would they try to take him away from Frannie?

Mari had to save Samuel.

Leaving the pail of milk on the ground, she scooped him into her arms and raced toward the house. Surprise gave her an advantage, and years of farm chores plus adrenaline racing through her body allowed her to outrun the stranger.

She yanked open the back door as he mounted the porch steps. With his fingers only inches away, she slammed the door and locked it. Then she collapsed against the solid wooden door and struggled to slow her ragged breathing.

RYAN JERKED his fingers back before she slammed them in the door. Why had he chased her? Now he'd alerted her to his presence, and both sisters would be on guard. He should have nabbed the boy outside the barn and run to the car. But his only job had been to ascertain the boy's whereabouts, not to grab him. He'd done his job. But he'd spooked one of the twins in the process.

Why had he gone over and talked to her? That had been

foolish on his part. He'd only intended to get close enough to identify the boy and make sure he wasn't being mistreated. From all reports, Frannie had a vicious temper.

As he approached the barn, he'd heard laughter—child's laughter—coming from inside. All he needed to do was conceal himself and study the boy after they emerged. But the sweet voice giving instructions and soothing the boy had mesmerized him and kept him standing in place too long. Using the mist as an excuse, he'd sneaked closer to the barn. The woman's sudden appearance had startled him. Instead of ducking behind the building, he'd approached her. An amateur mistake.

He'd made so many of them in the past two days. Sleeping outside the house last night had been another. He'd jolted awake each time a car passed, worried one of the twins would peek out the window and spot him or the police would arrest him for loitering. Before dawn, he'd moved the car in front of a neighbor's house, so the twins wouldn't see it when they woke for morning chores. Now he could barely keep his eyes open, but he had to call for backup, and then he needed to stay alert in case the sisters fled.

HER THOUGHTS WHIRLING, Mari kept her forehead pressed against the door and dragged in one breath after another, trying to fill her starved lungs with air.

Ruth stared at her in alarm. "Whatever is the matter?"

"A man," Mari gasped out. "Outside."

Ruth bustled over to the window and peered out. Her brow wrinkled into a puzzled frown. Then she turned to Mari. "There's no one out there."

"Are you sure?" Mari pushed away from the door and

went to stand beside her aunt. The porch was empty. Where had that man gone?

Ruth laid a gentle hand on her shoulder. "What happened?"

"A man was standing outside the barn when Samuel and I came out after milking."

Behind her, Frannie shrieked, "That blind man told people about us!"

Mari shook her head. "No, he didn't. He came to warn us yesterday that someone was asking about us."

Frannie's face contorted. "Why didn't you tell me?"

"I wanted to," Mari said, "but you seemed too upset to listen. I planned to tell you this morning."

"Now it's too late. They've found us."

At Frannie's shrill yell, Samuel huddled in the corner. Mari longed to cuddle him close, but she didn't want to draw her sister's attention to him. If Frannie discovered he'd gone outside this morning, she'd be even more upset than she already was.

"We have to get out of here *now*!" Frannie charged for the stairs.

Mari followed her. "What's going on?"

Her sister ignored her and pounded up the steps. Mari chased Frannie into her bedroom, where she began tossing clothes into her suitcase haphazardly. Her sister shoved everything down with one hand and tugged at the zipper until she managed to get it closed. Then she rushed toward the doorway, where Mari blocked her exit.

Setting her hands on her hips, Mari planted her feet and refused to budge when Frannie tried to shove her aside. "I'm not moving until you explain."

"There's nothing to explain. Evil people want to take Samuel away from me. And you blew our cover. Now get out of my way." Giving Mari a hard shove, Frannie elbowed her way through the door and bolted down the steps, calling, "Samuel, Samuel, where are you?"

Mari stood stunned. Her sister's jab to the ribs had winded her, but her words had been even more shocking. What did she mean? Why would anyone want to take Samuel from Frannie? That sounded like more than family members who didn't want Samuel raised Amish.

But she'd said *evil* men. Were they really evil, or had Frannie labeled them evil because they were coming to take away her child? When they were children, Frannie sometimes lost her grip on reality. Was that happening now?

Another thought struck Mari and stopped her cold. Suppose Frannie had done more than just yell at Samuel. Could that man be from Child Protective Services? Did he plan to take Samuel away?

Mari had to find out the truth. She raced downstairs to find Samuel cowering in the corner and Frannie trying to pull him to his feet.

"Come on," Frannie insisted.

"Wait." Mari caught her sister's arm. She had to slow her down and help her think logically. "You don't know if that man's still out there. You might be walking into a trap."

Frannie released Samuel's arm and gazed at Mari with wide, fear-filled eyes. "What are we going to do?"

Mari had no idea, but first they had to hear Frannie's story. Then they all needed to pray.

ALL DAY AT WORK, as Benuel greeted customers and made sales, a heavy cloud hung over him. Had he done all he could for Mari and her sister? Yes, he'd warned them about the stranger, but Mari kept coming to mind. Some of it was his initial attraction, but it went deeper than that. Almost as if God kept nudging him to take some action.

Benuel released a sigh after Susanna locked up at five. The internal tension had become unbearable. While his daughter counted bills and he rolled coins, he said, "When we're done here, I'd like to take out the team."

"I thought you might want to check on those ladies." Susanna reached for another stack of bills and resumed counting.

"What made you think that?"

"Well, you kept sighing. Oh, and you gritted your teeth a lot and looked worried. You did the same thing yesterday afternoon."

"I feel as if God wants me to help them, but I'm not sure how."

"Could we at least eat supper first?" Susanna snapped a rubber band around the stack. "Last night we barely had time to eat those sandwiches."

"If we make it a quick one." Benuel finished with the coins and slid them into the money bag. "Let's skip the usual cleanup. I'll come in early tomorrow to sweep and straighten up." By the end of the day, after customers had pawed through the goods, they usually left the shelves and bins in disarray. And today had been busier than usual.

Now all he wanted to do was to check on Mari. And Samuel and Frannie, of course. He hoped this urging came from God rather than his own desire to spend more time around Mari.

They closed the shop, and Susanna heated leftover chicken corn soup for supper. Benuel sliced and buttered bread to go with it. Following their usual silent prayer, they both ate hastily and ended with prayer as soon as they finished their meal.

Benuel rose. "I'll go hitch up the horse and lead him out front."

Susanna gathered the dishes. "I'll meet you out there once I've cleaned up."

By the time they reached Mari's road, the sun was low in the sky. Susanna slowed before Benuel's senses told him they'd arrived. A loud hiss of breath escaped from his daughter's lips.

"What's wrong?" Benuel asked.

"Why is that man from yesterday parked in that turnoff? He's just sitting in his car. Is he spying on your friends?"

"You're positive it's him?" Not that he needed any confirmation of his daughter's skill in observation. Since age four, Susanna had served as his eyes. She'd developed her sense of sight so she could describe things to him in great detail.

"For sure and for certain."

Her emphatic answer left no doubt in Benuel's mind. She'd seen the man for sure. But what did he want, and why had he parked nearby? Had Benuel been right to worry?

As they passed, Susanna slowed. "Hmm… It looks like he's sleeping."

"Sleeping?"

"Yes, *daed*, his head's back against the seat, his mouth is open, and he's snoring. Can't you hear him?"

Over the clatter of the metal-rimmed buggy wheels, a faint drone reached Benuel's ears. The man didn't sound as if he were faking sleep.

CHAPTER 7

When a team rattled into the driveway after supper, Mari froze. "Are you expecting anyone?" she asked Ruth.

Her *aenti* shook her head. "Not at this time of night. My friends come calling during the day."

A man emerged from the buggy. Without waiting to see if it was the man she'd run into that morning, Mari grabbed Samuel, rushed upstairs, and set him on the bed in her room.

"Don't make a sound," she warned him. "And don't come downstairs. Do you understand?"

His eyes solemn, he nodded.

She wished she had a toy or something to occupy him, but she'd get rid of the stranger as soon as she could. She raced back down the steps and arrived just as he knocked on the back door. Gasping for air after her brisk run, Mari inhaled deeply to even out her breathing and sent up a quick prayer.

Lord, please protect us. And give me wisdom about how to handle this situation.

She eased the door open, keeping a tight hold on it, in case the fake Amish man tried to push his way inside.

"Benuel?" Mari went weak with relief. "What are you doing here?" Then realizing how unwelcoming that sounded, she added, "It's good to see you. Come in, please." Nervously, she glanced behind Benuel and Susanna to be sure no one else stood on the porch behind them before she opened the door.

Susanna took her *daed*'s arm and signaled to him about the threshold. Mari waved her to the nearest chair, and Benuel ran his hands over the back before he pulled it out. He lowered himself into it, and Susanna sat beside him. Mari took a chair facing him, so she could study him uninterrupted. Ruth came around the table to sit beside her.

Mari called upstairs, "Samuel, you can come down. Frannie, do you want to join us?"

Tiny feet padded downstairs, but Frannie didn't answer. Samuel entered the room, then hesitated when he saw so many people at the table. Mari beckoned for him to come to her, and she pulled him onto her lap.

"You remember Benuel, don't you?" she asked.

Samuel nodded.

Benuel smiled in his direction, and Mari introduced him and his daughter to her *aenti*.

Ruth greeted him and then said, "I'm in a quilting circle with your mother-in-law. I was so sorry to hear of your wife's passing."

"Thank you." Benuel's husky voice revealed his sadness. "The past two years have been the hardest ones of my life. I couldn't have done it without God. And I've been so grateful for Susanna." He reached over and squeezed his daughter's shoulder.

Mari ached for them. Loneliness and grief were etched into the lines in Benuel's face as he spoke, and Susanna's eyes reflected her sadness and loss. More than anything, Mari wished she could reach across the table and erase their pain.

Some of Benuel's distress eased as he leaned forward toward Mari, but his face remained grave. "I felt a strong urging from God to come here today. As we approached your house, Susanna spotted the man I told you about yesterday."

Mari sucked in a breath. "You did?"

Susanna nodded. "He was sleeping when we passed, but his car is parked so he can watch your driveway."

"He must have been there all day." She told Benuel about her morning encounter. "Frannie refuses to tell me anything other than that evil men are after Samuel."

The little boy shivered, and Mari hugged him closer. "It's all right, Samuel. We won't let anyone hurt you."

"I'll do whatever I can to help," Benuel told her.

Mari was grateful for his offer, but what could he do? Maybe he'd know the answer to the question she'd been wondering about since that morning. "Would anyone be allowed to take Samuel away from Frannie? Like her husband's family?"

Benuel stroked his beard and appeared deep in thought. "I'm not sure about *Englisch* laws. I would think, though, if that man had a right to raise Samuel, he would have shown you some papers and taken the boy away."

"Yes, that would make sense." Mari's spirits felt a bit lighter.

And someone from Child Services would have identified himself. And he'd have proof—a badge or an ID cards or whatever they carried. She'd been too overwrought to think clearly.

"But why is this man watching the house? Do you think he intends to follow us if we leave?"

BENUEL DIDN'T ONLY THINK it was a possibility, he believed it was a certainty. Why else would the man be sitting outside all day? If they had a clue as to what he wanted, they would know better how to protect Samuel.

Mari interrupted his thoughts. "Frannie wanted to leave immediately, but I convinced her the man might follow us. I suggested waiting until after dark."

Benuel nodded. "A wise idea. But where will you go?"

"I have no idea. I'm leaving that up to Frannie. I'm not sure what her plans are."

"I'll be sorry to lose your company," Ruth chimed in.

"And I'll miss you," Mari told her. "After everything is settled for Samuel, I'll come back for a nice long visit."

"See that you do." Ruth folded her hands in her lap. "I didn't mean to interrupt. You'd better get back to your planning."

"I'm not sure what to do." Mari's voice shook slightly. "If he's waiting for us . . ."

"If he's still sleeping, now might be a good time to flee." Even as he said the words, Benuel's spirits plummeted. He'd barely had a chance to get to know her, and already he was losing her. He shook his head to dislodge that thought. If she returned to visit her *aenti*, maybe he could see her again. He wished she might consider friendship. Someone as sweet as she was would be able to find a husband who wasn't blind.

Mari shifted in her chair. Movements Benuel read as nervousness. "But how will we know if the man's still asleep?"

"Susanna and I could check. If he's awake, perhaps we could distract him."

Ruth waved a hand in the air, a motion that stirred a slight breeze. "You know, beyond those cornfields, there used to be a shortcut to the back road over the mountain. I don't know what condition it's in, but some of the *youngie* who have cars drive back there late at night."

"You mean we wouldn't have to go out to the main road?" The note of hope in Mari's voice tugged at Benuel's heart.

He wished he'd been the one who'd offered the shortcut. But perhaps he could provide some help. "If you and your sister need a place to stay, I have a cousin who runs a bed and breakfast on the other side of the mountain. She'd be glad to take you in."

"Oh, Benuel, thank you. I hadn't even thought about where we'd stay. I've been so focused on getting away."

So had he, but for a different reason. He wished she didn't have to leave. "Glad to be of assistance." The gruffness of his words covered the ache of losing her.

"Even if the shortcut is rough," Mari said, "it would give us a chance to get a head start. If we could leave without him knowing. . ."

"Don't worry. Susanna and I can keep him occupied."

"Thank you ever so much."

If Benuel never saw Mari again, he'd tuck that sweet expression of gratitude into his memory to warm his heart during cold, lonely days.

AT THE CRUNCH of wheels on gravel near his open car window earlier, Ryan had jerked awake. The heat from earlier in the day had plastered his hair to his forehead. His damp shirt stuck to his back. How long had he been sleeping?

If those women had whisked the boy away while he slept, he'd lose all his pay. And he'd look like a fool.

The girl driving the buggy looked like Benuel's daughter from that secondhand shop. What were they doing all the way out here? *Obviously, Benuel had been the one who'd warned the women about me.* Their wagon turned into the driveway of the house.

When Benuel didn't return right away, Ryan relaxed. The shopkeeper wouldn't stay if the women had left.

Ryan's nap had refreshed him, and he could stay up all night again if he needed to, although they'd promised him backup around ten tonight. Once they came, he could check into a hotel and sleep for as long as he wanted.

After an hour, Ryan got antsy. He hopped out of the car to stretch and pace around. Maybe he should check to be sure Benuel was still there. Dusk descended as he headed toward the house, staying close to the cornfields. Whenever a car engine growled in the distance, he ducked into one of the rows and waited until it passed. Then he resumed his walk. He also hid from buggies. The last thing he needed was some gossipy neighbor warning them of his presence.

He reached the property. Benuel hadn't left yet. His buggy remained parked near the barn. One of the shadowy figures inside the house appeared to be Mari. Three people sat at the table. The man on the right had to be Benuel. His daughter sat beside him. The person beside Mari seemed to be an older lady. A small figure crossed the room. The boy.

Upstairs, framed in a window overlooking the driveway, an indistinct silhouette blended with the wall. That had to be Frannie.

Perfect. Everyone was still here. Ryan could go back to his car and wait for reinforcements to show up. Although he didn't have a good view of the house from his car, he could see the end of the driveway. If the women left, he'd be able to follow them.

~

MARI SCRAPED her chair back from the kitchen table. Benuel's plan had given her hope. And her pulse still fluttered from the heart-stopping smile he'd directed her way when she'd thanked him.

"I'd better go tell Frannie we need to pack the buggy." She shifted Samuel in her arms. He was almost asleep, so she set him on the couch and covered him with a light blanket.

Twenty minutes later, they assembled in the kitchen with their bags around them. Ruth stood at the counter preparing food and snacks she insisted on sending with them. Frannie, edgy and tense, paced back and forth, her lips pinched together as if holding back a verbal explosion.

Her own stomach in knots, Mari stood by the door, staring out at the dark lawn they'd need to cross. She hoped they could transfer Samuel, who was sleeping, to the buggy without waking him. Keeping him quiet would be one key to their escape. The other would be limiting the noise the buggy made. Benuel suggested driving over the grass for as long as possible.

Behind her, a chair scraped back, and footsteps shuffled in her direction. Benuel's outstretched hand brushed the back of her arm, and tingling shot through her. Mari closed her eyes and hoped he couldn't hear the rapid thumping of her heart. Or if he did, that he'd attribute it to her worries for Samuel.

"Mari?" Benuel's velvety soft voice soothed her. "I wish I could go with you, but I'll be praying."

"*Danke*," she whispered, choking back a lump in her throat. Because he couldn't see her smile, she leaned over to pat his arm.

He reached out with his other hand and covered hers. "Everything will work out fine. God is in control."

"Yes, He is." Her heart pitter-pattered at the warmth of his touch. Now that she knew he was single, she couldn't help wishing they'd had a chance to get to know each other.

"Why don't I help you hitch up the horse before Susanna and I serve as a distraction?" Benuel's breath near her ear sent shivers down Mari's spine. "If you don't mind holding my arm?"

Mari stopped herself from blurting out, *I'd be delighted.* Instead, she tried to act calm. "Of course."

She hated losing his hand over hers, but after she took his arm, he reached across with his other hand and covered hers again. Being this close to him made it difficult to breathe.

"We'll be right back," she told everyone.

As they crossed the lawn, Mari watched for anything that might trip him up. Once or twice on the uneven ground, he stumbled slightly and pulled her nearer. Her heart galloped faster than a wild pony. Mari wished this time together would never end.

They laughed and joked quietly as they dragged the buggy from the barn. Mari marveled at how sure and strong Benuel's hands were. He seemed to instinctually know where to move, and in a short time—much too short for Mari—they'd finished hitching up the horse.

She snuggled a little closer than necessary on the way back, but Benuel didn't seem to mind. In fact, she got the impression he liked it. Mari's heart sank as they reached the house. Would she ever see him again? Had God brought them together, only to pull them apart?

"I'D BE happy to help carry out the luggage," Benuel offered, hoping to prolong their time together. Once everything had been stowed, and he'd accompanied Mari to the buggy as she carried Samuel, he released her arm with great regret so she could place the small boy into the back seat.

Now that the buggy was packed and ready to go, Mari would soon be driving away and out of his life. He tried not to think of that but instead savored each moment with her while they waited for Frannie.

After Frannie climbed into the driver's seat, Benuel took Mari's hand in both of his. "God be with you. I'll be praying for everyone's safety." He repeated his cousin's address. "If you wait about five minutes before you take off, I'll be sure to keep that man from leaving."

"*Danke*." Mari withdrew her hand from his but laid a gentle hand on his arm. "Be careful."

He didn't expect the man to be dangerous, but it was sweet of her to care. "I will, and you do the same. I hope we can meet again sometime."

"I do too," she whispered, giving him hope.

Susanna took his arm and led him to the buggy. As thankful as he was for his daughter's help, he missed Mari's soft hand. He had to find a way to see her again, but with the shop open six days a week and church every other Sunday, it seemed an impossibility. Meanwhile, he'd pray for her every day.

Susanna turned around and headed for the road. Benuel bowed his head and asked for guidance in dealing with the man in the car.

"He's awake, *daed*," his daughter said.

"Can you pull across the turnaround so you block his exit?"

"I think so." Susanna turned the horse sharply to the right and proceeded at an angle. "I don't think he can get out, but now he definitely can't see across to Mari's yard."

"Are you able to see them?" Benuel's anxiety spilled over into his words.

"Not from here. And the house is dark."

"Good." According to plan, Ruth must have gone upstairs to bed. Now if only the rest of the arrangements went as smoothly.

"Can you take me over to the car so I can talk to him?"

"Of course." The buggy shifted slightly as Susanna slid the door open and hopped out.

After Susanna tied the horse to a nearby telephone pole, they strolled over to the car.

"Good evening," Benuel said casually as if they'd just happened to notice him in passing. "Fancy meeting you out here."

"Um, yes. Well, I was just sitting here, um, admiring the view."

"You must be a true lover of farms and fields then? Susanna mentioned seeing you here when we passed earlier."

"I, um, fell asleep."

"I see." Benuel stroked his beard. They'd definitely made him uneasy. Good, maybe he'd hightail it out of here and forget about spying on Mari and Frannie. "Do you often sit on country roads to nap? When you're not staring at scenery, that is?"

"Not really. I—" The man took a deep breath. "Look, I think we both know what I'm doing here. You were in the house, so one of the twins must have told you she saw me this morning."

"Actually, she did. I believe you frightened her and the little boy."

"Yes, well, I can't tell you why I'm here, but whatever she told you isn't the truth."

"Originally, I guessed an abusive husband was stalking her, but you don't seem bent on revenge."

"Me? Her ex?" the man squawked. "Not hardly."

"So you're stalking her for someone else."

"Believe me, there are no abusive husbands involved. You can go home and relax."

Benuel had no intention of going home or of leaving here until he'd given Mari enough time to get away. "Then what are you doing?"

"I can't say." A stubborn streak underlay his words.

"They're worried you're going to take the little boy."

"I have no intention of taking him."

Benuel listened for the slight tremors that indicated a lie, but the man's answer was smooth, with no hesitation. Yet something about the way he'd delivered that sentence set off an alarm. Had he emphasized the *I* slightly?

"No relatives of her deceased husband are trying to take the boy away?" In addition to stalling this man, Benuel hoped to learn more. It would make it easier to help Mari and Samuel.

The man's laugh was cynical. "Look, I don't know what story they concocted, but things are not what they seem."

"What do you mean?" When the man didn't answer, Benuel kept pressing but got nothing more out of him.

The man pointed to the darkened house. "Looks like they went to bed."

"*Jah*, it appears that way." But in reality, only one person had. "Perhaps we all should too."

"Good idea." But the man made no move to start his car.

Benuel didn't want to leave until the man did, but he did want to be sure Mari and her sister had gotten away safely. "Come, Susanna, we should go."

His daughter led him to the buggy. He prolonged their walk by inching along and pretending to stumble several times.

Susanna giggled softly and whispered, "If you're trying

68

to make that man think you're incompetent, you're doing a *wunderbar* job."

"*Gut*," he muttered. And we're giving Mar—" He stopped abruptly. "I mean, we're giving the twins more time to get away."

His daughter gave his arm a playful squeeze, letting him know she'd caught his slip. She didn't seem bothered by it, which was promising.

He struggled to get into the buggy.

"Don't overdo it, *Daed*," Susanna warned.

Leave it to his daughter. She could be as canny as he was. Although that made him proud, it also concerned him.

As she climbed in, Benuel tried to identify what was bothering him. The conversation had left him with a vague sense of uneasiness. Someone was lying. And he didn't think it was Mari.

CHAPTER 8

*C*louds obscured the moon, providing additional cover as Frannie eased the buggy over the rutted grass. The wheels creaked and rattled, but Mari hoped those noises blended into the night sounds of crickets chirping, owls hooting, spring peepers chirping, and corn stalks rustling.

Once they were hidden by the cornfields, they bumped over rough, uneven ground. Near the top of the hill, they passed two cars hidden in a stand of trees at the far edge of the field. Mari hoped they belonged to *Englischers*, but they might be teens during *Rumschpringa*. She prayed they'd use wisdom and not do anything they shouldn't.

After jouncing along on the rutted path for at least ten minutes, it was a relief to turn onto the narrow mountain road. Frannie flicked the reins, and the horse picked up speed.

"Be careful," Mari warned as the horse broke into a gallop. "This road is winding and has no guardrails."

"Stop bossing me around," Frannie snapped. "You

always think you know best. We need to get away as quickly as we can. If those men find us. . ."

The way her voice trailed off left Mari with a feeling of dread. "Who are they, and what do they want?"

"None of your business." Frannie glowered at Mari.

Although she wanted to caution Frannie to keep her eyes on the road, Mari worried about enflaming her sister's temper.

Frannie's driving grew even more reckless and erratic as the buggy climbed to the crest of the bluff. The sheer drops on both sides of the road made Mari's stomach quiver. The carriage swayed back and forth.

Finally, Mari couldn't stand it anymore. "Frannie, slow down. Or let me drive."

With a maniacal laugh, Frannie spurred the horse faster and yanked on the reins to overcorrect for an unexpected twist in the road. The horse tried to stop, but the weight of the buggy was too great. They plunged over the edge.

"Jump!" Frannie screamed as the horse struggled to get its footing. She shoved her door open and leaped out.

Mari yanked her door open, but she couldn't go without Samuel. As the carriage careened from one side to the other, she reached over the seat and clutched Samuel.

A violent jerk tossed them both from the buggy. Wrapping her arms tightly around him, Mari shrieked as she hurtled headfirst downhill on her back. Wind rushed past her ears. Jagged sticks and sharp rocks jabbed her, tearing into her dress.

"God, please help us!" she screamed.

Clinging to Samuel with one arm, she flailed desperately, grabbing for roots or saplings to slow their fall. Her body twisted sideways, and she landed with a thud on a narrow ledge.

Dizzy and disoriented, Mari lay, aching, sore, and

bleeding. But Samuel was safe. He wailed and tried to wriggle free.

"No," she shouted. "Stay still." They lay inches from the edge. A sheer drop yawned below them. The tiniest movement could send them plunging over the edge of the cliff.

She ran one hand over Samuel's back as he sobbed.

"Mom," he wailed. "Want Mom."

"I know," Mari soothed. "We can't move, or we'll fall. Your *mamm* will come soon."

His cries quieted to whimpers as she repeated her assurances that *Mamm* would come. On the hill above them, Frannie struggled to unhook the horse from the overturned carriage. The buggy lay crushed against the trunk of a huge oak. Had Button been hurt?

Mari prayed. For her safety and Samuel's. For her sister. For the horse. For their rescue.

Frannie peered down the slope at Mari and Samuel lying precariously on the ledge. A calculating expression crossed her face, and without saying a word, she turned and climbed the hill, without making an effort to help.

From where Mari lay, she could see her sister lead the horse up the steep incline. Frannie didn't appear to be limping or bleeding, but Button hobbled beside her. Mari hoped her horse had no major injuries.

When her sister reached the top, she tried to mount Button, but the mare squealed and reared, knocking Frannie to the ground. Frannie wailed, scooted away from the horse's hooves, and pounded the ground with her fists. Then she crumpled in a heap under a nearby tree.

Mari called out, trying to attract her sister's attention. She didn't know what Frannie could do, but at least she could comfort her son, who was trembling in Mari's arms. Had he glimpsed the ground far below them?

Maybe Frannie staying up near the road might be best—on the slim chance she might attract the attention of a passing driver.

Alone on a deserted road late at night, how likely would it be that a car might pass by? They could be stuck here until morning.

BENUEL COULDN'T PUT his finger on what bothered him about this man, but Mari should be far enough away to be safe. And if this guy sat here all night waiting for them to wake, he'd be sorely disappointed tomorrow morning.

As Susanna clicked to the horse to start him moving, a car engine growled closer. It seemed to be crawling down the road and slowed even more as it neared.

"*Daed*," his daughter whispered, "that man is talking into his phone. And so is the passenger in that car coming toward us. He's looking all around here. Do you think they're talking to each other?"

The car rolled past slowly. The engine slowed to an idle.

"They're stopping near Ruth's house."

"Go down the road a little way and turn around. Then let's drive past Ruth's and pull into the neighbor's driveway." Benuel didn't want to leave Ruth alone. "Could you see who was in the car?"

"It looked like two men—both *Englischers*."

No more Amish imposters? What did these men want with Mari and Frannie?

After Susanna turned, she slowed the horse to a walk to go past Ruth's. She sucked in a breath. "That car with the two men inside is in the driveway. Guess whose car is parked behind theirs?"

Benuel didn't need to guess. He'd followed the sound of

RACHEL J. GOOD

both car engines. Should he get out and confront the men? He really didn't want Susanna there with him, but he'd need her help to walk over to them.

His daughter had more news. "All three of those men are standing on the front porch."

"Keeping driving past. Once you pull in the neighbor's driveway, let's get out and cut through the cornfields. Maybe we can reach the back of the house without them seeing us."

He knew one thing about most of the Amish in this area that the *Englischers* didn't. Most of the Amish didn't lock their doors. He prayed Ruth hadn't tonight.

If she'd gone to bed, it would take her a while to dress. He might have enough time to help when she went to answer the men's knock.

The buggy wheels crunched over gravel when Susanna turned the horse into the driveway. "How far should I go?"

"As soon as we're far enough up the driveway that they can't see us, let's tie up the horse and go to Ruth's back door. And I want you to wait for me on the back porch." Benuel had no idea what those men wanted, but he didn't want his daughter involved.

After Susanna tied up the horse, she took his arm. They crept along, keeping close to the cornfield so they could duck between the rows if the men looked their way.

With Susanna keeping watching, they darted across the yard. "Don't worry," she assured him when they reached the back of the house. "They didn't see us. They were too busy pounding on the door, looking annoyed."

Benuel climbed the stairs to the porch. "Go hide in the barn," he whispered. "That might be safer."

"*Daed*," she protested.

"Please, Susanna, I don't want you getting hurt." Although she sighed, he waited until she rustled through the grass, heading away from him.

74

Then he jiggled the back door handle. He'd been right. The knob turned.

He stepped inside and eased the door shut. Shuffling overhead indicated Ruth was getting ready. He didn't want to startle her or alert the men to his presence, so he waited until she came down the stairs to call out quietly.

Ruth sucked in a sharp breath and clutched at her heart. "Oh, Benuel, you scared me."

"I'm sorry. I don't know who those men are on the front porch, and I didn't want to leave you here alone to face them."

"I should be fine. God is with me."

"Yes, everything is God's will, but sometimes he sends others to help us."

"You're right." Ruth sounded relieved. "I wish I knew what was going on. Thank you for being here. If I need you, I'll call out." She strode to the front door and opened it.

Benuel hid where he could hear.

"FBI, ma'am."

"Yes, I see that from your badges." Ruth's voice stayed calm and unruffled.

"We'd like to speak to the two young women staying here."

Benuel's blood pounded in his ears. FBI? What did they want with Mari and Frannie? There must be some mistake.

"I'm sorry," Ruth told them. "The girls left earlier today."

"That's not what our informant told us. He's been watching the house, and no one has left."

"I assure you they have."

"Ma'am, we have a warrant to search the house."

"You're more than welcome to do that." Ruth opened the door wider and motioned for them to come in.

They ordered Ruth to stand outside and left the fake Amish man to guard her.

But Ruth didn't seem cowed. "I just *redded* up before bed. Please don't make a mess in there." She sounded like a mother scolding naughty children.

Benuel snickered to himself as he shuffled quietly to the back door, eased it open, and shut it soundlessly behind him. Ruth could take care of herself.

If only he hadn't sent Susanna to the barn. They needed to hurry.

"*Daed?*" she whispered close to his ear.

Benuel jumped.

"I didn't mean to scare you. I thought you'd sense I was here."

He'd been too tense and worried about Mari to pay attention to anything. He could have walked into all kinds of danger. "You were supposed to be in the barn."

"I couldn't leave you alone in there. What if you wanted help? Or what if you came rushing out the door and needed me?" She added a touch of sarcasm to her final question.

"I'm not going to scold you now. You're in the right place at the right time. Thank the Lord."

Lights went on in several rooms. The men must be searching the house. He and Susanna had to get out of here before anyone spotted them.

Benuel grabbed his daughter's arm, and they rushed to the cornfields for cover, then made their way back to the buggy.

As soon as they were both inside, Benuel pointed to the right. "And turn left at the next crossroad. We need to get on the mountain road Frannie took. Go as fast as you can, as long as you're driving safely."

He had to warn Mari about the FBI. While Susanna drove, Benuel explained about the men at Ruth's house.

Neither of them could figure out why the FBI was searching for Mari and Frannie. The FBI didn't help relatives take children away from their mothers, did they?

Unless. . .

A new idea niggled at him. Suppose Frannie had lied. What if her *Englisch* husband wasn't dead? Benuel had read about custody disputes in the newspaper. The Amish didn't face such problems because they didn't divorce, but it seemed rather common among *Englischers* for a parent to take off with a child. If they crossed state lines, would the FBI get involved?

The more Benuel thought about it, the more likely it seemed. Frannie came across as short-tempered and unkind. And Samuel seemed tense and fearful. Perhaps a judge had decided she wasn't a fit mother.

He ran his theory by Susanna.

"You could be right. Ruth mentioned Frannie had been living in Maryland."

Benuel disliked taking a child away from his mother, but even he had to admit, if he were the judge, he wouldn't want to give Frannie custody.

Now Benuel was torn. He'd planned to warn them about the FBI, but what if Samuel's life was in danger?

After they'd driven two miles, Benuel directed Susanna to take the right fork at the next intersection and head over the mountain. He hoped this was the way Mari had gone. As they crested the first hill, shrieks split the air.

"*Ach*," Susanna cried. "It's Frannie, and she's alone." A few seconds later, Susanna pulled the horse to a stop. "Oh, no, their carriage is crushed down there."

Were Mari and Samuel in it?

"Hurry, Susanna. I need to get over there to help."

"Nobody's in the carriage, *Daed*."

As soon as she'd secured the horse to a tree, she circled

the buggy and took his arm. "Be careful," she warned. "There's a steep drop-off near the edge of the road."

As they approached, Frannie's shrillness signaled hysteria, but for some reason, it struck a wrong note. Something sounded off, puzzling Benuel. Why would she feign distress?

"Are you all right?" Benuel called as they headed in her direction, but Frannie didn't answer, only increased her volume.

With a tinge of disgust, Susanna said, "She doesn't look hurt."

"Susanna," Benuel reprimanded her. "Did she hear you?"

"I don't think so. She's standing up and brushing leaves off her dress. And she's fake screaming," Susanna confided the last part in a low voice that, if his hearing hadn't been so keen, Benuel might not have heard over Frannie's piercing cries.

"Does she look upset?" he whispered.

"Hardly." Susanna's dry tone made it clear Frannie was playacting. "Her eyes are shifty."

"Where's Mari?" Benuel demanded of Frannie when they reached her. "And Samuel?"

Between sobs, Frannie choked out, "They fell out of the buggy and rolled down over the cliff."

"What?" Benuel's whole body went numb. *No!* He couldn't have lost her. Was he destined to lose everyone he cared about?

Susanna clutched his arm hard. "I think something's moving on that ledge down there." She tugged him to the right.

"I have to go down to check."

"You can't, *Daed*. It's much too steep."

"I need to try. If it gets too dangerous, I'll belly crawl."

"No, *Daed*, please don't do this. I can't lose you too."

Benuel pulled her into his arms and hugged her. They'd both been through a terrible loss. He understood her fear, but he had to rescue whoever was down there. He only hoped they weren't too badly hurt. "I need to go, but pray for me and for Mari and Samuel."

"What can you do? You can't see." Frannie's strident comment followed Benuel as he started down the slope. He grabbed a sapling and clung to it as he swished his feet through the debris and fallen leaves that carpeted the dirt and rocks until he found a foothold. Then he moved lower. Inch by inch. Foot by foot. Tree by tree. Guided by Susanna's directions from above until her voice grew too faint to hear. Then he went by instinct and prayer.

LEAVES CRUNCHED NEARBY, and Mari tensed. A wild animal roaming the woods? Would it attack them?

Please, God, help us, she prayed over and over, sometimes silently and other times aloud.

"Mari?"

The first time she heard the voice floating on the wind, she thought she'd imagined it. Then it came again faintly.

"Benuel?" Could it really be him? Or had she hit her head so hard on her tumble onto the ledge she'd been knocked out?

"I'm coming, Mari. It's slow going. I can't afford to be careless." Benuel's words rang out. "If I make a mistake, Susanna says I could plunge off the edge. Then I'd be no help to you."

Loose dirt and pebbles showered down on her and Samuel. The little boy cried out.

"Don't move," she begged Samuel. "Stay very still. Someone's coming to get us."

Benuel's foot wriggled in the air above her, and she screamed, "Stop!"

He chuckled. "Don't worry. I could tell I'd reached the edge." He scrabbled back up a bit. Leaves rustled as he changed position.

He must have turned around and crawled toward them, because next thing she knew, he ran his hand along the edge. Then his head appeared.

Mari gazed him with gratitude, but he'd never know. With Benuel, she needed to put everything in words—or touch.

The tears in her eyes also clogged her throat. "*Danke* for coming."

"No need to thank me. Are you both all right?"

"I-I think so."

She ached all over and would be covered with scrapes and bruises if she made it out alive. As if sensing her thoughts, Samuel quieted. His soft, hiccupping gulps assured her he was calming. And he hadn't complained of being hurt.

Benuel's forehead creased in concentration. "I want to help you, but you'll have to direct me."

"Don't worry about me. Please take Samuel."

"Is there a way I can get down to you?"

"*Neh!* I don't think this ledge will hold more weight." Bits of it already had crumbled and fallen, and she worried it might give way entirely if she or Samuel moved too much. But saving the little boy had to be her only priority.

Despite trying to act composed, worry edged Mari's words. "We're about eight feet down, but I can't stand up. Not with Samuel."

"If I anchor myself up here and reach down, can you lift him up?"

"I'll do my best."

Praying hard, she directed Benuel to slide to the left until he was directly over where she'd be lifting Samuel. She waited while Benuel hooked one foot around a rocky outcropping and the other on a sturdy sapling.

"Can I reach him from here?" he asked.

"I-I think so." As long as his footholds supported him and the extra weight. If they didn't, he'd plunge over the bluff.

Benuel appeared to be fearless, but perhaps not knowing the depth of the drop helped him stay calm.

Remaining flat on her back, the way she'd fallen, Mari grasped Samuel by the waist. Slowly, inch by inch, she lifted him into the air, rotating him slightly so he faced Benuel.

Her muscles burned as she held him aloft. Mari prayed she could raise him high enough. And that her arms wouldn't give out.

"Want Mom," he whimpered.

"I'll take you to your *mamm*." Benuel spoke in a soft, reassuring voice.

Although she panicked inside, Mari kept her tone as gentle and soothing as Benuel's. "Samuel, hold your arms up so Benuel can reach you."

Body rigid and eyes wide with fear, the small boy did as she said. Seeming to sense Samuel's location, Benuel moved slightly in that direction, leaned over, and extended his hands.

Mari's arms trembled and burned under the strain. If they gave out, Samuel would plummet—

Stop! Don't think about that.

She concentrated all her energy into scooting near enough that Samuel could grasp Benuel's outstretched arms.

Each time she shifted position, small bits of ground crumbled away underneath the ledge.

Please, Lord, I'm not asking for my life, only that You keep Samuel safe. Don't let the ledge give way until he's safe.

Searing pain shot through Mari's arms and shoulders as she lifted Samuel a few more inches. His fingers almost brushed Benuel's. "Reach higher, Samuel. Try to grab Benuel's hands."

Mari prayed harder than she ever had in her life, begging God to connect their hands. To let Samuel live.

When the small boy's fingers brushed Benuel's palms, Benuel leaned down farther and stretched until he could grasp Samuel's wrists. Mari blew out a breath. *Danke*, Lord. They'd done it.

Now came the most dangerous part. Mari prayed Benuel's footholds were sturdy enough to support the extra weight and that his arms could bear the sudden burden.

"When I let go," she reminded him, "you'll be bearing his full weight. Let me know when you're ready."

Strong and confident, his words floated down to her. "I'm ready."

Mari's chest constricted with admiration and fear. One false move, and they could all be lost.

"Don't be scared, Samuel." She hoped her voice didn't give away her own terror. "Think about Mommy."

Then she let go, and Benuel tugged the boy toward him. Another chunk of dirt gave way under the ledge. She prayed the narrow shelf would hold.

Benuel grunted at the sudden weight on his arms, and the small boy swung like a pendulum in the air. Samuel shrieked and kicked.

His muscles visibly straining, Benuel pulled the little boy to him. After several tense moments, Samuel was close enough for Benuel to drag him onto solid ground. Then

Benuel wrapped his arms around Samuel and drew him close.

In unison, Mari and Benuel both exhaled loud, drawn-out sighs. And Samuel's keening quieted.

"Get Mommy," he whimpered.

"We will," Benuel promised and bent to kiss the boy's tousled curls.

Tears trickled down Mari's cheeks. What a *wunderbar* man! So brave and caring.

Benuel, with Samuel cradled close to his chest, still had a long upward trek as he scooted backward over the rough terrain that had scratched and torn Mari's skin and clothes. But the worst was over.

"I'll be back for you," Benuel called out.

Mari wasn't sure the ledge would hold that long, but she thanked God Benuel had rescued Samuel.

BENUEL SHUFFLED up the steep incline at a painfully slow pace. He probed the ground ahead of him with one foot before he took each step, and he tested the sturdiness of every vine, tree, or sapling to be sure it could support both their weights. Cradling Samuel left only one arm free to pull them upward.

All the while, Benuel's thoughts remained on Mari. He couldn't give in to exhaustion. He had to make it to the top as quickly as possible so he could go back and rescue her.

In the distance, sirens screamed, coming nearer. Had Ruth told the FBI where to find them? On the road above him, piercing blares blasted through the air as police cars screeched to a halt. Radios squawked and hissed static. To Benuel, the cacophony was deafening.

He struggled up the last few feet and sensed chaos and a

milling crowd. Probably police officers or FBI agents. Strong arms snatched Samuel from Benuel's arms.

"That's him," Frannie screeched nearby.

A beefy man, judging by his viselike grip, hauled Benuel up to flat ground.

"Let me go." Benuel struggled to free himself. "A woman's trapped down there. I have to save her."

A gruff voice said, "Let him go. We'll send someone down with him to get her."

As soon as the other man's hold loosened, Benuel wriggled away. Nothing would stop him from reaching Mari. "I can do it," he insisted. "I got the boy."

The thought of these strangers touching Mari bothered him. Benuel wanted to rescue her himself. He clutched a jagged stump, prodded the rugged forest floor behind him with one toe, and took a step back. Then another. He'd been up and down this slope before. This time, he'd do it faster. He turned around and had gone a few feet before someone snarled at him to stop.

"Rogers," a man barked, "grab a rope and follow him."

Benuel didn't have time to wait. The ledge Mari lay on was precarious. Several times when she'd moved, rocks and clods of mud tumbled down into the valley below her. What if the shelf broke off completely?

In his rush, Benuel miscalculated. His foot slipped, and he crashed to the ground. He dragged himself upright using a sapling, his heart still pounding from the sudden fall.

He had to slow down and go cautiously. He'd be of no use to Mari if he fell. He tested and double-tested each foothold before setting his weight on it.

When he was partway down, someone above him began the climb downhill, sending showers of dust and pebbles over him. "Wait," he shouted. "Dirt's getting into my eyes."

"Sorry." A sharp odor of fear mingled with sweat rose from the man who stopped a few feet behind Benuel.

"I can do this myself," Benuel assured him. "I got the boy. I can get her too."

"Might be best for only one of us to go. Do you want my rope?"

Something thudded beside Benuel. He bent down and grasped the thick, rough coil of rope. Draping it over his shoulder, he resumed his descent. The closer he got to Mari, the harder he prayed. He'd barely been able to hold Samuel's sudden weight as the little boy dangled over the edge of the cliff. How would he support Mari?

After what seemed like an eternity, he neared the ledge. "Mari?" he had to shout to be heard above the bedlam above them.

"I'm here," she called back.

Benuel's heart leapt in his chest. The ledge hadn't crumbled away before he reached her. He hoped it would stay intact while he rescued her. "I'm going to toss you a rope. Can you secure it around your waist?"

"I'll try."

He threw the rope in the direction of her voice.

"Too far to the left," she said.

Each time he threw, Mari gave him instructions for getting it closer. Never once did she exhibit any impatience with his clumsiness. "If only I could see," he yelled in frustration as the rope missed its mark again.

"Thank God you can't," she retorted. "You'd probably never have come down this steep incline."

Humbled by her words, Benuel apologized to God for criticizing how he was made. Then he concentrated on imagining Mari's location and seeing the rope floating toward her. Maybe it would make more sense to lie down and dangle the rope over the edge. Why hadn't he thought of that before?

He lowered himself onto his stomach, and she coached him where to move.

"Almost," she said. "A little more to the right."

The relief in her voice cheered him. They were going to do it.

Suddenly, an avalanche of rock rumbled down the cliff. It sounded as if it came from Mari's ledge.

"Are you all right?" he called.

"I sat up to grab the rope." Her voice vibrated with fear. "But I dislodged some of the ledge."

Please, God, help me to rescue her before that ledge falls apart.

CHAPTER 9

*M*ari clung tightly to the rope as Benuel secured it around a sturdy tree. Then slowly she eased it around her waist. Each movement sent pebbles and earth cascading down into the chasm below.

"Mari?" Benuel's voice trembled.

"I'm still here," she replied, her voice shaking even more than his. The ledge could give way at any moment and send her spiraling into space. But she didn't want to worry him.

"Keep talking to me so I know you're safe," he begged.

Her throat dry, Mari prattled on about how she was securing the rope, ignoring the ominous rattle of falling debris under her. She prayed aloud as Benuel edged nearer, and she directed his movements to get him as close as possible without endangering him.

"Can you lift your hands over your head and keep a grip on the rope?" Benuel asked.

"I think so. . .if I can move slowly, without jarring the ledge too much." She sounded shaky. "I'll let you know when I'm ready." With every miniscule move, Mari chattered to let him know she was still on her precarious perch. "I'm in place."

Benuel rechecked his footholds to be sure they were strong and secure. "I want to be sure they'll hold the extra weight." Then he lay on the ground again. After a prayer for her safety, he announced. "All set. I'm going to start pulling."

The first hard tug on the rope yanked Mari almost upright. Half the ledge cascaded down into the gorge. She lost her footing. Fear paralyzed her throat and strangled her scream.

The rope jerked her to a stop. Stomach queasy, Mari swung back and forth in empty space. She closed her eyes so she couldn't see the ground so far below.

"Are you all right?" The alarm in Benuel's tone matched the panic roiling her stomach.

Only a gurgle made it through her lips.

Could anyone possibly be all right when they were dangling in the air with nothing preventing a plunge except a piece of twisted twine? Twine that might fray and drop her to her death.

Desperately, she clung to her thin lifeline.

The rope juddered as Benuel hauled it upward. Painful flames engulfed her muscles. The roughness of the rope bit into her skin and chafed her palms, but she kept her death-grip on her only chance of survival. And she prayed and prayed.

Mari squeezed her eyes shut and blocked out the rest of the nightmare. The swaying movements, the collisions with the cliff face that scraped her elbows and forearms raw, the jittering between upward yanks. Even her trembling limbs, her raw and blistering palms faded into blankness and mumbled petitions to the Lord.

"We're . . . close . . . now, aren't . . . we?" Benuel panted between words.

She opened her eyes, and his face appeared. What a blessed sight!

"Only a foot or so more," she choked out.

"Praise . . . the . . . Lord!"

With a tremendous tug, he dragged her up until her torso flopped onto solid ground. Benuel wrapped the rope around the stump to be safe, then he extended his arms.

When his fingers wrapped around her wrists, she let out a small sob. Benuel groaned and drew her into his arms. She wrapped her arms around him and rested her head against his chest, her heart echoing his rapid, erratic beats. Her joy overflowed when he bent his head until his lips almost touched her hair.

"Oh, Mari," he breathed.

Then his gentle fingers explored her face. "At last, I get to see what you look like." His featherlike caress whispered over her forehead and eyes. He brushed the tears from her cheeks, traced a finger over her lips and chin, and then cradled her close.

As lights flashed and sirens whirred around them, Mari melted against him. Her hero. He'd risked his life to save her.

Cameras clicked and flashed. Benuel shielded her face with his hand and ducked his head until his forehead rested against hers.

"Please don't take pictures," he called out.

"Hey, guys," someone yelled, "the Amish don't allow picture-taking. It's against their religion."

"Can't take pictures of the kid. Can't take pictures of the hero. Can't take pictures of the criminal," someone else grumbled.

Benuel offered her his hand. "I guess we'd better climb the hill to find out what's going on."

Despite her palms being rubbed raw in places, Mari took his arm. She never wanted to let go. With him keeping them safe by hanging onto trees and her guiding the way, they struggled up the slope together.

Their faces grim, two officers approached.

Mari's heart seized in her chest. "Was my sister hurt when she fell from the carriage?"

Instead of answering, the policewoman moved behind Mari and grabbed her wrists. Cold metal clinked. Encircled her wrists. Her raw palms, aching arms, and bleeding back faded into the background.

"Frannie Johnson, you have the right to remain silent," the other began.

"Wait! I'm not Frannie. That's my sister. What's going on?"

The male officer ignored her outburst. "Anything you say can and will be used against you. . ." His voice droned on, and as soon as he finished, the female officer pushed Mari forward with a firm hand on her shoulder.

"There's been a mistake. Where are you taking me?"

The policewoman steered into the backseat of a squad car.

Mari's whole world had turned upside down. First, she'd hurtled downhill in the buggy, then Benuel's tender touches had set her heart and mind whirling, and now reality tilted yet again. She'd be tempted to think she was dreaming, but the metal cuffs bit into her wrists, and a cage in front of her blocked her off from the front seat.

Outside the window, Benuel argued with the other officer. Rotating lights threw red stripes across his face, and though fear paralyzed her muscles, Mari couldn't help admiring him. Not only had he saved her and Samuel, now he was fighting to set her free.

~

"Please," Benuel pleaded with the officer. "The woman you're arresting is Frannie's twin. Her name's Mari. She's done nothing wrong."

In a bored voice, the policeman asked, "This is the one who was in the buggy with the little boy when it went over the embankment, right?"

"Yes," Benuel agreed. "But what does that have to do with it?"

"She's on the FBI Wanted List. She matches the description, and we have her picture."

"That can't be." Benuel would stake his life on that. Mari was honest and true. He trusted her completely. He, who could tell when people lied about their bills, wouldn't have been fooled by an imposter. "You've made a mistake."

The officer snorted. "That's what they all say."

Although Benuel hated to incriminate Frannie, he had to do something to cast doubt on Mari's arrest. "How do you know you have the correct twin?"

"Talked to the other one. She gave us all the information."

"She lied." Benuel couldn't believe Frannie would frame her sister, but perhaps the officers who heard her story misunderstood.

"She's right behind you. Why don't you ask her?"

"Frannie?" Benuel whirled around. "They've arrested Mari. Tell them the truth."

"The truth about what?" If voices could have sneers in them, Frannie's certainly did. "I think you're mixed up, Benuel. I'm Mari."

"No, you're not." He'd know Mari's voice anywhere. And he'd recognize her sister's.

With fake sweetness, she cooed, "It's an understandable that you can't tell us apart when you can't see."

Benuel felt as if he'd stumbled into a bog filled with quicksand and each step drew him deeper into the mire.

This couldn't be happening. How could he prove Mari's identity?

A hand descended on his shoulder. "You're a hero, man. Nobody can believe a blind man could rescue two people on that dangerous terrain."

Benuel would recognize that voice anywhere. *The fake Amish man.* He whirled around, and his hand snaked out to grab the other man's arm. "Who are you? And what's going on here?"

"My name's Ryan Stevens. Guess it can't hurt to tell you the rest now that they've wrapped up the case." He shook off Benuel's hand. "I'm a private investigator. This was only my second job, so I made some amateur mistakes, but we still nabbed our quarry."

"Then you're the one who's responsible for Mari's arrest. You have to tell them they made a mistake."

"What are you talking about, man? They arrested Frannie. The kidnapper."

Benuel stood stock-still. "Frannie's a kidnapper?"

"Yep, she snatched the kid she babysat for and transported him across state lines. That's why the FBI's involved."

Benuel tried to make sense of this information. Samuel wasn't Frannie's son? The other day in his shop, Benuel had guessed she wasn't a grieving widow. But he couldn't process the rest. Only one thing stood out in his mind. The police thought Mari was a kidnapper.

He gripped Ryan's arm again. "They've made a mistake and arrested the wrong sister. They have Mari, not Frannie."

"Nah, it's all OK. Mari's standing right over there by a tree. No worries."

"You don't understand. Frannie lied. She told them she was Mari."

"What proof do you have?"

Benuel had no proof. Only his own observations. "I can tell them apart."

Ryan laughed. "You probably can. With the way you figure things out about people, I'd believe that."

"You have to convince the police they made a mistake. Ask them to arrest Frannie before she gets away. Please, Ryan. If they take the wrong sister, Frannie will be free to kidnap another child."

"You'd better be telling the truth, man. My future's on the line here."

"Just get them to arrest Frannie before she gets away."

"Will do."

A short while later, Ryan returned. "They're holding Frannie, but they want you to come and identify the twins." He took Benuel's arm and accompanied him to the police car. "Both twins are standing across from us."

"This guy's blind," one of the policemen said. "How's he going to tell them apart?"

"I hope you're not going to rely on his testimony." Frannie's cynical voice.

Benuel had no trouble recognizing it. He pointed in her direction. "That's Frannie."

"You jumped to conclusions without seeing them or touching them or anything," a policeman scoffed.

"I don't need to. I can hear the difference in their voices."

"But only one spoke."

Benuel gritted his teeth. He had to prove this to them. "Switch their places around several times, so I don't know which one is where. Then have them each say the same sentence. I'll tell you who is who."

As shuffling ensued by the squad car, Benuel took a deep breath. He had no doubt he'd pick the right one, but would the officers be convinced?

An officer ordered both women to say *I am Frannie.*

Mari's sweet voice was first, but Benuel held his tongue. Frannie went next and adopted Mari's dulcet tones, but her words contained a note of underlying belligerence.

He pointed to the left first. "That's Mari." Then he swung his finger toward the right. "And that is Frannie."

"I couldn't hear any difference in their voices." The policeman's skeptical tone made it clear he didn't believe Benuel.

"I didn't either," a policewoman agreed. "But he did point out the same person both times."

"Believe me," Ryan said, "he's spot on with his instincts. He told me so many things about myself just from listening to me. You have to believe him."

PLEASE BELIEVE HIM, Mari pleaded silently.

"You're going to take his word when none of you could tell the difference between us?" Frannie scoffed. "Besides, she's the one who had the little boy."

"That's true," the officer holding Frannie's arm said.

Mari's eyes stung. When they'd been children, Frannie sometimes had lied to get Mari in trouble. But falsely accusing her of breaking a plate or stealing a handful of cookies was nothing compared to placing the blame on her in a criminal case. Mari didn't even know what Frannie had done. She only hoped the arrest was a mistake.

"What's going on?" Her voice shook. She had no idea what they thought she did.

"Mari," Benuel answered, "Frannie kidnapped Samuel."

His words made no sense. "Samuel's her son." You couldn't kidnap your own son.

"No, she babysat him, and she transported him across state lines."

"I-I don't understand." She turned to Frannie. "You said your husband died, and Samuel—" Was his name even Samuel? He wasn't Frannie's son or Mari's nephew. "He's not my nephew?" her voice faltered. The enormity of what Frannie had done washed over Mari.

"Good try, Frannie." Her sister sneered at her. "Your little act almost sounds convincing."

Act? Mari's stomach churned. Her sister was determined to blame her. *Please, God, show me what to do.* Despite Frannie's actions, Mari's heart flooded with love for her sister. Although human love might fail, God's love never did. And Mari could depend on His love to see her through.

She whispered the words of I John 1:9 so only her sister could hear. "*If we confess our sins, he is faithful and just to forgive us our sins, and to cleanse us from all unrighteousness.*"

Mari hoped the words would touch Frannie's heart. Her sister might not be able to get out of the punishment she deserved according to the law, but she could get right with God, which was the most important thing.

Her sister glared at her, but Mari prayed the Lord would touch Frannie's heart.

"Where's Susanna?" Benuel asked. "She's seen Frannie and Mari. She can tell them apart."

Mari searched the area. Susanna sat huddled in the buggy. "She's in your carriage." When Benuel hesitated, she added, "It's directly behind you."

He pivoted and beckoned for his daughter, who hopped out and hurried over.

Susanna hugged him. "I'm so glad you're all right. I

prayed the whole time you were gone that God would help you rescue Mari and Samuel."

"Why did you stay in the carriage?"

"Frannie was going to steal it. And then I stayed inside when the photographers came."

"*Tsk, tsk.*" Frannie gazed at Mari and shook her head. "Stealing a buggy? After you kidnapped that little boy, Frannie?"

"I'm not Frannie," Mari burst out. Her sister was messing with everyone's minds. Who knew she could be such a great actress?

Susanna stared at Frannie. "Huh? You're Frannie." Then Susanna drew in a quick breath. "Did you hit your head in the accident?"

"*Neh*, I'm fine." Frannie smiled sweetly at Susanna. "It's easy to get us mixed up when you only saw us once."

"You might not know or remember, but I saw you more than that. And I spent time with Mari." Susanna gestured toward Mari.

The officer holding Frannie frowned. "Seems to me everyone's pointing out the same person."

Benuel smiled in Mari's direction, and she was grateful for his support. But if everyone had seen her and Benuel together after the rescue—her face heated at the thought— would the officers assume Benuel was fingering the wrong person to keep her out of prison?

CHAPTER 10

*A*n older officer cleared his throat and directed his comments to the policewoman holding Frannie. "Even if everyone identifies the woman you're holding as Frannie, we still need proof to detain the real culprit. Facts we can use in court."

"Can't really use DNA," the policewoman commented. "Identical twins are too similar."

An FBI agent in a black suit strode over to join them. "But their fingerprints are different."

"Yeah." The older officer nodded. "Guess we'll have to take both of them to the station for prints."

"I'll have my team send our records." He took a phone from his pocket and tapped rapidly. "We dusted Alexander's house for fingerprints, so once his parents arrive and we know which twin is Frannie, we can wrap this up."

Only Mari noticed the fear in her sister's eyes.

A short while later, a car drove up and screeched to a halt. A man and woman jumped out. Samuel screamed and broke away from the policewoman holding his hand. "Mommy! Daddy!"

They both bent down and swept him into a group hug. "Oh, baby," his mom said, tears streaming down her cheeks.

"Well, if you don't believe Benuel or his daughter," Ryan said, "why not ask the parents? They should recognize their babysitter."

One of the FBI investigators strode over to the parents. After speaking to them for a few minutes, he led them over to the sisters. Samuel had his arms entwined around his father's neck as if he'd never let go. His mother kept one hand on his back.

"We'd like you to identify your babysitter please," the investigator said.

Both parents studied Mari and Frannie, their faces contorted in anguish. Finally, the father spoke, "They look so much alike, don't they? And I've never seen Frannie in Amish clothes, but I'm pretty sure she's the one." He glowered and pointed to Frannie.

His wife looked back and forth a few more times, a sick look on her face. "I agree." She pointed to Mari. "That sister"—the woman's face twisted—"isn't as skinny as, as. . ." She spat out the name with venom, "Frannie."

"I don't want to traumatize your son, but could he make an identification as well?" When they nodded, the investigator said to their son, "Alexander, can you point to the woman who took you away from your home?"

Alexander. The little boy she'd been calling Samuel had a different name. Mari remembered his words in the secondhand shop the other day. *Not Samuel.* He'd been trying to tell her that wasn't his name, and she'd misunderstood. How many other clues had she missed? Those poor parents must have gone through such agony. All because of her sister.

Alexander lifted his head from his father's shoulder and glanced at Mari. When their eyes met, he smiled. At least he didn't hold it against her. And when she'd told him his mommy would be waiting for him at the top of the hill, she'd been mistaken. But his real mommy had come.

When he turned toward Frannie, he shrank back and emitted a cry. Then he buried his face against his father's shirt.

One of the FBI men motioned to Mari. "Let her go. I think we have the correct suspect."

Mari winced as they unlocked her handcuffs. Her hands were raw with rope burns. Her arms and shoulders ached from lifting Samuel and from clinging to the rope. And from having her hands behind her back.

"Where will they take Frannie?" Mari asked as they put her sister into a squad car.

"She'll be tried in Maryland because that's where the family lives," the policewoman answered. "And that's where she committed the crime."

"I'll have to find a ride so I can be with her during the trial."

Benuel stepped up beside her and slipped an arm through hers. "I'm so sorry about Frannie." He paused before adding, "I'd be happy go with you."

"Thank you, Benuel. And not just for offering to go along. I can never thank you enough for what you did tonight."

"Oh, I'd say you did a pretty good job of thanking me earlier," he teased.

Mari's cheeks heated, but at least she didn't have to worry about Benuel noticing. "I'm so grateful. You saved my life and Sam—I mean, Alexander's. I still can't believe how courageous you were."

"Perhaps if I could see, I might have been too frightened to do it."

"I'm so glad it was you who rescued us." Recalling

Benuel's arms around her, holding her close made her breathless.

He swallowed hard. "Me too. We should get you checked out by the paramedics first, but then I have something I'd like to ask you."

"Do you want to wait here while I go over to the ambulance?" Mari asked.

"Definitely not," Benuel emphasized his words. "If I had my way, I'd never let you go anywhere without me again."

That would be just fine with Mari. There was nowhere she'd rather be than beside him.

After an EMT cleaned Mari's wounds and applied antibacterial cream, she shook her head. "You're lucky this is all that happened in that fall."

Mari sent up a prayer of gratitude. "God protected me."

"And you did a wonderful job protecting that little boy. He only had a few minor scratches."

"I'm so glad." Mari prayed Alexander would heal quickly internally as well. And that her sister would too.

"Speaking of brave," Benuel said as they walked away to find the private spot he'd requested, "that EMT was right. You were amazing. Even when that ledge began to collapse, you didn't hesitate. You insisted I take Alexander first."

"I only did what I felt God leading me to do."

Mari stepped into the woods and behind some trees. "Is this private enough?"

"If we're alone and no one can see us, then it's private enough for me."

"These huge old oaks will shield us from everyone's view." Most of the police cars and emergency vehicles had driven off.

"We can't stay long, because Susanna might worry, but I hope you'll let us drive you back to Ruth's."

"Thank you. We'll need to get the horse back, too." He

nodded, and Mari's hopes plummeted. He wanted to be alone to say that?

"We can manage the horse, but that's not what I wanted to ask. I wondered. . ." The nervousness in Benuel's voice made Mari ache for him. "That is, if you're staying in the area, would you let me court you?"

Court her? He wanted to court her? She'd been hoping he'd hug her again, but this? This was joy beyond measure.

Benuel shifted from one foot to the other. "Mari?"

She hadn't meant to make him wait for her answer. Her heart had shouted *JAH!* the minute he'd asked.

Her lips curved into a smile. "The answer is *jah*. Yes, I'd love to." She snaked her arms around his neck and, with the backs of her aching hands, lowered his head to hers. "You couldn't see my smile, so I thought I'd help. In case you had trouble finding my lips," she murmured.

Benuel cupped her face in his hands. "I'll never have any trouble with that," he assured her as he ran a tender finger over her lips. Then he wrapped his arms around her, bent his head, and pressed his mouth to hers.

Mari's spirit soared. She'd found a home. Right here in Benuel's arms, close to his heart. And in the town where he lived. She hoped Ruth had been serious when she'd invited Mari to stay for a long time. Because Mari intended to stay here forever and ever.

THANK YOU FOR READING THIS NOVELLA

I'm grateful you chose it. I hope you enjoyed traveling to Lancaster County Amish country, and I pray the story uplifted and blessed you.

If you enjoyed this story, I hope you'll read my Amish novels.

The links below will take you to my pages:

Website: http://www.racheljgood.com

Amazon author page: https://www.amazon.com/Rachel-J-Good/e/B019DWF4FG

Facebook: https://www.facebook.com/racheljgoodnovels

Thank you ever so much!

Rachel

P.S. If you'd enjoy learning more about the Amish, you're welcome to join my private Facebook group, the Hitching Post:

https://www.facebook.com/groups/196506777789849/

And if you haven't already, you can sign up for my newsletter at http://bit.ly/1qwci4Q

ABOUT THE AUTHOR

RACHEL. J. GOOD

USA Today bestselling author Rachel J. Good writes life-changing, heart-tugging novels of faith, hope, and forgiveness. She grew up near Lancaster County, Pennsylvania, the setting for her Amish novels. Striving to be as authentic as possible, she spends time with her Amish friends, doing chores on their farm and attending family events.

Rachel is the author of several award-winning, bestselling Amish series in print or forthcoming – *Love & Promises*, *Sisters & Friends*, *Unexpected Amish Blessings*, and *Surprised by Love*, along with two books in *Hearts of Amish Country* – as well as many anthologies, including *Amish Christmas Twins* and *Christmas at the Amish Bakeshop* with Shelley Shepard Gray and Loree Lough. She is also the coauthor of the *Prayerful Author Journey: Inspirational Weekly Planner*.

Rachel hosts the Hitching Post, an online site where she shares Amish information and her book research. She also enjoys meeting readers in person and speaks regularly at book events, schools, libraries, churches, book clubs, and conferences across the country. Find out more about her at: http://www.racheljgood.com

Connect with Rachel

Hitching Post
Newsletter sign-up

Facebook
Goodreads
Pinterest
BookBub
Instagram

ALSO BY RACHEL J. GOOD

HAVE YOU READ THEM ALL?

∾

SISTERS & FRIENDS series

Change of Heart

When her younger sister goes wild during *Rumschpringa* and dates an *Englischer*, Lydia Esh teams up with his older brother to break up the couple. But she doesn't count on falling for an *Englischer* herself. Will Lydia stay true to her faith if it means giving up the man she loves?

Buried Secrets

Emma Esh has recovered physically from the accident that almost claimed her life, but she has no memory of the year before the accident, so she has no idea why her sister tries to keep her from falling in love with their next-door neighbor Sam Troyer. But an unexpected visit from an old boyfriend and the gradual return of her memory tears Emma's life and romance apart.

Gift from Above

Sarah Esh's peaceful life is torn apart when a parachutist crash-lands on her family farm and begs her to keep his presence secret because his life's in danger. That promise tangles her in a web of deceit that endangers innocent people, ruins her best friend's reputation, and tears apart the Amish community. Sarah must confess and repair the damage she's done, but how can she admit the truth to Jakob Zook, knowing it will end their relationship?

Big-City Amish

After Abner Lapp's betrayal and his choice to leave the Amish community, Rebecca Zook tries to forget him, but how can she ignore his mother's plea to watch his four young brothers during her cancer treatments in New York City, even if it means being around Abner? Rebecca's tender heart won't allow her to ignore him when he's hurting, but she can't let herself fall for him again, especially when he's not right with God.

∿

LOVE & PROMISES series

The Amish Teacher's Gift

A teacher at the Amish school for children with special needs, Ada Rupp struggles to balance her job with caring for her seven orphaned siblings. She has no time to date, but she'll do anything in her power to help her young student, Nathan Yoder, and his grieving widowed father.

The Amish Midwife's Secret

When Amish midwife Leah Stoltzfus insists on using herbal remedies for her patients, sparks fly between her and the new *Englischer* doctor, Kyle Miller. In more ways than one. Can they overcome their differences to rescue a pregnant teen and save her unborn baby?

The Amish Widow's Rescue

After Grace Fisher's husband dies unexpectedly, her neighbor, the reclusive Elijah Beiler, offers to help with her animals and household repairs just to be neighborly. He has no intention of getting entangled with the pregnant widow or her children; he's been hurt enough in the past. But he hasn't counted on Grace's young son, who's determined they need a new daddy.

UNEXPECTED AMISH BLESSINGS series

His Unexpected Amish Twins

When Micah Miller becomes the guardian of his twin niece and nephew after their parents are killed in a buggy accident, he's grateful for Hope Graber, owner of a horse therapy farm, who helps all three of them all deal with their grief. Hope makes them smile again and wins a place in Micah's heart. But will his deep-seated fears and Hope's close partnership with her *Englisch* trainer keep them apart?

His Pretend Amish Bride

Priscilla Ebersol has no chance of marriage after her boyfriend's humiliating rejection ruins her reputation, but after she helps an Amish camel farmer in a nearby town and she's mistaken for his wife, Priscilla's matchmaking *mamm* sees this as the perfect opportunity. Unfortunately, her meddling might drive the couple apart instead of together.

His Accidental Amish Family

Following a buggy accident, Anna Flaud is told she'll never walk again. She refuses to accept that and spends years recovering, and she's also working toward becoming a foster parent. Then she's offered a chance to fulfill her dearest wish—motherhood—by adopting three siblings with special needs. But it comes with strings attached: she needs a husband. Her exercise therapist, Levi King, would be perfect for the role except Levi can't trust himself to care for one child, let along three.

～

SURPRISED BY LOVE series

Unexpected Amish Proposal

After Fern Blauch loses her market stall, Gideon Hartzler offers to share his stand with her, but once they start working together, will her rival in business end up as a rival for her heart?

Unexpected Amish Courtship

Isaac Lantz, who trains Labrador retrievers as guide dogs, is enamored with Sovilla Mast, who sells homemade dog food and treats. Gaining a dog's affection is easy, but bashful Isaac has no idea how to win the heart of the woman he loves.

Unexpected Amish Christmas

To help himself recover after a buggy accident, Jeremiah Zook pens inspirational letters to grieving families mentioned in the Amish newspaper. Moved by the letter he's sent, Keturah Esch corresponds with him. Little does she know, Jeremiah has a nearby market stand. When he shows interest in her, she rebuffs him because her heart belongs to the anonymous letter writer. A Christmas gift accompanied by a letter might just hold the key to both their hearts' desires.

Amish Marriage of Convenience

When widower Stephen Lapp moves his five children from New York State to Lancaster County, Pennsylvania, his only plan is to buy his family's farm stand. But on Stephen's first trip to the market, his brave act of kindness nearly ends in catastrophe—until strong-willed Nettie Hartzler saves him—and makes an impression he can't forget. Nettie has no interest in getting involved with any man. But when Nettie runs into serious money worries and Stephen proposes a marriage of convenience, she's distressed and conflicted. She's come to know Stephen's gentle heart and generous soul, but will he marry her if she reveals her dark past?

Her Pretend Amish Boyfriend

Noah Riehl has dark secrets in his past that prevent him from marrying a faith-centered Amish girl like Caroline Hartzler. But when she needs a fake boyfriend to discourage a persistent suitor, who won't take no for an answer, he agrees to rescue her. But will his kindness lead him into the very relationship he's vowed to avoid?

Dating an Amish Flirt

Everyone accuses Rachel Glick of being a flirt because she's caused several breakups and broke many hearts, but she only wants to spend time with her brother's friends after his death. Josh Yoder wants to help the grieving family, and God seems to be leading him to Rachel. But with her history of breaking hearts, is she the right choice?

Missing Her Amish Boyfriend

Anna Mary Zook is struggling to cope with her new job at the market and care for her five younger siblings as Mamm spirals into another depression. Abe King longs to be there for her, but he can't leave his aging father to run their New York state farm alone. Can Abe and Anna Mary find a way to be together?

~

ANTHOLOGIES

Amish Christmas Twins, ***Christmas at the Amish Bakeshop***, ***Amish Christmas Kinner*** (with Shelley Shepard Gray and Loree Lough)

Amish Christmas Miracles, ***More Amish Christmas Miracles***, ***Amish Spring Romance*** (with Jennifer Beckstrand, Jennifer Spredemann, and others)

Amish Across America (free; with multiple authors)

Amish Christmas Cookie Tours (with Mindy Steele and Jennifer Beckstrand)

Love's Truest Hope (with Mary Alford and Laura V. Hilton)

Love's Thankful Heart, ***Plain Everyday Heroes***, ***Love's Christmas Blessings***

(with Laura V. Hilton and/or Thomas Nye)

~

NOVELLAS

Amish Christmas Treasure, ***Amish Mistletoe & Miracles***, ***Amish Wedding Day Revenge***, ***Amish Twin Trouble***, ***Missing Amish Daughter***, ***Amish Secret Identity***, ***Amish Thanksgiving Strangers***

~

OTHER TITLES

Amish Quilts Coloring Book (regular and large-print versions)

__Prayerful Author Journey: Inspirational Weekly Planner__

Hearts Reunited in *__Hearts of Amish Country series__*

Love's Secret Identity in *__Hearts of Amish Country series__*

Check for more Rachel J. Good titles <u>here</u>.

Made in the USA
Monee, IL
22 July 2024